Nice Men
Finish Last

Nice Men Finish Last

PRAVESH VIR SIDDHU

Srishti
PUBLISHERS & DISTRIBUTORS

SRISHTI PUBLISHERS & DISTRIBUTORS
Registered Office: N-16, C.R. Park
New Delhi – 110 019
Corporate Office: 212A, Peacock Lane
Shahpur Jat, New Delhi – 110 049
editorial@srishtipublishers.com

First published by
Srishti Publishers & Distributors in 2017

To Mummy and Papa,
For your continuous support.

"In the end, we all complete our life's jigsaw puzzle, but the void once created always stays. Some live with the void and some spend their life in search of the missing Piece…"

— Pravesh Vir Siddhu

Acknowledgements

Nice Men Finish Last came into existence with the help and support of the following people. I begin with thanking Muneet, a very dear friend, whose unwavering encouragement helped me bring this book to life.

This book was written over a period of time. Every day I wrote some and mailed the content to Muneet, who read each chapter with great enthusiasm and waited eagerly for other chapters to come. Her interest and eagerness motivated me to continue writing every day. Her criticism, however, did the opposite. But it helped me to better myself. Muneet, honestly, every page of this manuscript was written to impress you. Hopefully I continue to do the same.

A big thank you to my father Vir, for passing on his creative wisdom to me and for teaching me that imagination has no limits. My mother Gita, I am so gracious for everything you have been. Thank you for believing in me long before I believed in myself. I am grateful to my sister Silvi, who set the bar so high that it encouraged me to push myself further. Silvi, you are my role model and one day I wish to become as inspiring as you.

I cannot imagine this creative journey without my friend with paws - Romeo, who sat patiently beside me as I tapped my fingers on the keyboard during the dark hours of the night. Buddy, you sacrificed as much sleep as I did for this project. Your unconditional love kept my spirit and creativity alive.

My appreciation also extends to these three wonderful institutes: ITS Dental College, Indraprastha Dental College and Cambrian College, that helped create timeless memories predominantly with these four friends – Vipul, Shalin, Saurabh and Ramneek. Thank you for always having my back.

Nancy, Charu, Prekshya and Patrick – you guys were the first ones who said I could, therefore I should write. Thank you for believing in me. My accolades to Srishti for her enticing vocabulary, some of which became part of this book (Next time, try claiming copyright!).

I would also like to extend my appreciation to Dr Sonali Taneja and Dr Manju Kumari, the two teachers who churned the creativity within me. (I still doubt I was graciously awarded above passing marks in lieu of my creative showcases.)

My dear friend Meet, thank you for reading the synopsis at the very last minute and giving me your valuable feedback. Emma, can't thank you enough for re-motivating me and always being there, every time I doubted myself.

Last, but not the least, I would like to thank Jayanta da and Arup at Srishti Publishers for believing in the idea, and Stuti for refining the manuscript with her editorial talent.

To send in your observations or feedback, write to me at praveshvirsiddhu@gmail.com.

Game Over

"Dhoni finishes off in style. A magnificent strike into the crowd. India lift the World Cup after twenty-eight years…"

With these words from Ravi Shastri, one billion Indians began to cheer in joy. One billion jumped into the air to celebrate. One billion, but one… I was the only one who wasn't included. I was on the ground, lying subconscious and battered, and covered in blood.

It was the 2nd of April 2011 and I had decided to meet my girlfriend who had been ignoring my phone calls for over a month. Her name was Noor; she was as bright as her name, and attended the neighbouring engineering college. We had been together since our high school days. Everything was going great until she cheated on me. She was now secretly dating a guy from her own college. I was kicked out of her heart, but I could not tolerate that. And the worst part was that I was kept in the dark about her secret affair. I discovered it through her roommate Swati, who was once my good friend.

It was the 2nd of April and I was determined to go to her campus and talk to her. I chose this day for two reasons – one, she always complained that I preferred cricket over her. Sparing time on the very important evening of the World Cup final would prove that she was more important to me than cricket. Secondly, I wanted to avoid contact with her much stronger new boyfriend. I say this as he is a big cricket fan and I knew he would be busy that evening, so it would be the opportune moment.

As the Sri Lankan innings ended at 267/6, every Indian anxiously sat in front of the television screen. Some were praying to god, some were fasting, some had faith in superstitions and some had painted their faces in the tricolor. I was also anxious, not for India's chase, but about my chase for Noor. I wanted to talk to her and express my love to her once again.

"I want to meet Noor. Can you fix a meeting for me please?" I said to Swati over phone.

"Why don't you understand? She has moved on and it is better that you do too," Swati replied.

"I don't want your advice. I want you to fix a meeting with Noor."

"Any meeting with Noor will be a meeting with Danny."

"I don't care about him. I want to talk to Noor at any cost."

"You don't know Danny. He is big, muscular and strong and influential, and he is not as nice as you are," Swati reasoned.

"You think I don't have muscles? I am not strong enough?" I said angered and I flexed my biceps. I saw the size of the miniscule bulge that popped out. It seemed like even my poor biceps were laughing at me and asking me to calm down. Logic soon took over and I realized that Swati was right – these muscles would do me no good.

"Do you really want me to answer that question?" Swati said, as she knew I was not even close to strong.

I calmed down and took a deep breath.

"I am already emotionally damaged. My body has stopped feeling pain. Do you think I care about physical pain anymore?"

"Oh god!" Swati scoffed. "Come out of the fairy tale."

"I cannot forget her." My voice broke down as I said that.

"Okay, don't cry. I will try my best. I will bring her to the cafeteria. You will only have half an hour to talk to her. Okay?"

"Only half an hour!" I shouted, disappointed.

"Don't be grumpy. It is more than enough. I can make her sit there all day but that is how far Danny lives from the campus. If she calls him, he will be there in half an hour. And I don't want you to discover your stronger side."

Swati hung up. I had strictly thirty minutes to speak my heart out in front of Noor. Only thirty minutes to speak thousands of unspoken words.

That meant I had to chase an ODI target with the speed of T20. I accepted the challenge. To add to the impact, I wore a blue shirt that Noor had gifted me when we were together. The Indian innings began as Virender Sehwag and Sachin Tendulkar walked to the crease. I began my chase as I entered the neighbouring engineering college. The two men in blue took the guard. This man in blue walked inside the campus without any guard.

Since it was difficult to stay away from cricket, I plugged in my earphones and tuned into the radio to listen to the live commentary. India lost the first two wickets in quick succession. Swati messaged me from cafeteria that I needed to hurry up because Noor didn't want to stay in the cafeteria for too long. I had less than thirty minutes now. The target had become tough.

"The required run rate is very high and the target seems tough at this stage." The commentator shouted inside my ears. It seemed like he was describing my situation. "The batsmen need to settle down and stabilize the innings."

I took the instructions from the commentator and entered the cafeteria where Noor was enjoying a sandwich with Swati, totally unaware of what was coming her way. They both were sitting right in front of the television. The cafeteria had only a few people who were not much interested in cricket, but were still cheering the men in blue.

I sat right in front of Noor, my back towards the television.

"Hi," I said smiling.

Astonished, Noor gave me a blank expression. She looked at Swati seeking an answer. Swati replicated the same blank expression.

"How come you are here?" Swati asked to break the ice.

"I was stalking Noor," I said to make Noor laugh. She smiled a little and bowed her head down.

It was a good start. I was proud of myself. Another person who appreciated me was the commentator. "That is a very intelligent stroke from the youngster. It seems like the men in blue have taken control over the innings after the few early blows."

I tried to strike a conversation, but the pitch was not favouring me at all. Noor dug her eyes on the sandwich and her fingers fidgeted with it.

"Please talk to me Noor. I came here only to express how much I love you. How much I miss you. I don't know what went wrong between us, but…" I went on and on and on.

I was warned by the commentator, but I didn't listen to him. "He needs to slow down here. There is absolutely no need to play such kind of shots at this stage."

I played some bigger shots, unnecessary at this stage.

"What happened to us?" I stepped out of the crease to rant. "We were like Romeo and Juliet of our high school. What went wrong? I won't let this partnership end. We are like Gambhir and Kohli." I gave reference to the two set batsmen on the crease. "We are in this never-ending partnership that does well even in pressure situations."

Noor smiled again. Swati giggled too. It was working. I stepped a few more steps out of the crease and took a chance. I exceeded the analogy to an extreme level.

"We will take India home. You are aggressive like Gambhir and I am like the youngster Kohli. A little immature, but learning every day. It is impossible to end this partnership."

"It is in the air and Virat Kohli is gone. There was absolutely no need to play this shot." The commentator shouted and Noor looked at me for the first time.

Then through her eyebrows she pointed towards the television screen.

"This partnership has come to an end. India needs to find a balance now." The commentator advised.

Noor made it clear that I had made too many mistakes which had led to the end of this partnership. It was time for me to find a balance and let her go. But I was stubborn, destined to make more mistakes.

"Indian captain takes his stance. India has to perform a miracle if they have to win this world cup," the voice from the TV boomed.

I took my stance and fought back.

"Noor, we can start afresh. It is never too late to make a new beginning."

Noor continued her pretence of indifference. Her fingers were still fidgeting with the sandwich on the paper plate. She had not uttered a single word since I sat in front of her. Luckily, she had not called Danny yet, which meant I had some more time.

I had to be careful. I had to be patient. Being continuously ignored by Noor was stealing that patience. The fact that a half-bitten stale sandwich had more attention than me was getting on my nerves.

"Talk to me. Look at me. That sandwich won't talk back to you," I said as I put my hand over hers. This was probably the last mistake I could have made. Her reaction surprised me. She flicked my hand away, wrapped the sandwich in the paper plate and threw it at me. I ducked down in the last moment. It scared the hell out of me and Swati too.

Noor got up from the chair and left the cafeteria. I took some time to gather myself and darted towards her.

Swati suggested not chasing her. She tried to hold my hands to stop me.

"Can't you see? She is not interested at all!" Swati yelled.

"Didn't you see my defence? That is how well I am prepared." I imitated the ducking down to flying sandwich.

"Noor," I shouted as I ran behind her.

She stopped right in front of the girls' hostel guard room. Entry beyond this point was barred for me. She decided to settle the matter here.

"Can you please leave? I don't want to talk to you," Noor yelled.

The guard stepped out. "Any problem, bitiya?" he asked, lowering down the volume of his radio which undoubtedly was tuned to the live commentary.

"No uncle, I am alright. Thanks," she replied politely.

The guard stood there for some more time pretending to adjust the signals on his transistor.

"Can you step away from this guard room?" I didn't want to come across as a stalker.

We walked towards the engineering college central ground. The mildly cold breeze began to fan the surroundings. I was still able to listen to the commentary from the transistor, but for the first time I ignored what the commentator was saying. I got into my own zone and tried to persuade Noor again.

"I love you Noor. I know you asked me to stay away for some time. I tried, and trust me, that place is not beautiful without you. I need you in my life. I need you for everything. I need you for…"

"I don't need you," Noor said interrupting me in between. "I had told you this before and I am telling you again. I don't love you and I don't need you at all, for anything."

"But why? What did I do? Just because I got a little bit busy in my studies? It was you who pressured me that we've got to get married as soon as possible. I was working towards it. I am not an engineer. It is not a cakewalk for me."

"You mean to say college was cakewalk for me? I didn't study enough?"

"You did. But I am the one who has to ask your dad for marriage. I am the one who has to be good enough for your parents to say yes."

The arguments continued back and forth. We both yelled at each other. We both grunted. We both tested each other's patience. As the night was getting quieter, we were getting louder.

At this point. Noor was completely unaware that I knew about her new affair. When my patience gave up, I made another mistake.

"When were you going to tell me about Danny? When were you going to tell me that you are cheating on me?" I said calmly.

There was silence. I clearly heard the commentator say, "And a superb stroke from the man in blue and the ball flies to the boundary."

"Good that you brought him up yourself. Thanks for taking that burden off my shoulders," Noor replied.

"You know that you have done something very unethical and very wrong. That is why you call it a burden."

"Nothing is wrong or unethical. He cares for me. He knows how to treat me right. He…"

"Can you shut up?" I yelled. Noor praising someone else was highly intolerable. I was furious.

"That is what you can do. You can only yell at me. The biggest coward I've ever met in my life."

"Shut your mouth," I said as I grinded my teeth. "Just because I am non-violent does not mean I am a coward."

"Tell this to someone who doesn't know you. You cannot even protect me."

"Protect you?? Are you a monument that I have to protect you?" I fought back.

"Exactly! Danny thinks I am a monument that needs to be protected. It would be better that you leave. If he finds out that you were yelling at me, you cannot imagine what he will do."

"Are you trying to threaten me?"

"It is not a threat; it is an advice to save your life. You can call it an emergency manual," Noor replied sarcastically.

"And you think I am scared of some random guy who stole my girlfriend from me? Call him. Let me see what he can do."

"He stole your girlfriend!" she said venomously. "That is why you should have protected her."

She took the phone out of her pocket and dialled a number. She wanted me to ask her to stop perhaps. I knew it would result in an apocalypse, but I stood unmoved. Before pressing the call button on her phone, she once again looked at me and asked for my assurance.

"Go ahead," I said in a firm voice.

"Hey sweetie, can you come to the central ground?" she said in a cheesy manner to tease me.

He declined the offer initially; must have been watching the match. But Noor knew the power she had.

"There is a bug in my laptop that is bugging me. Can you come and take care of it?"

That was probably the engineering code language that I was unaware of.

She hung up the phone and smiled at me.

"Fifteen more minutes. Any last wish?" she said to tease the bug.

"How can you do this to me? I didn't expect this from you."

"Tsk tsk tsk," Noor made a pitiful face. "The little baby is scared."

"Shut up, you cheater. You are the worst person I've ever met," I said in agitation.

"Keep going, I am listening."

Nothing I said bothered her, as she was too busy mocking me. I was scared, but I knew these were my few minutes to see Noor, to talk to her and to be around her. Noor's presence was enough to overcome that fear. But fear has funny ways of expressing itself. In my case, it flowed out from the eyes. I squatted on the ground and cried helplessly. I cried partly because I was scared and partly because I had not expected Noor to be this heartless. The girl who once cared was laughing at my pain.

"I loved you Noor," I said as I squatted on the ground, hiding my face in my palms. "I loved you a lot. I could not express it properly."

"It is too late now. I cannot do anything. Stop creating a scene here."

"It looks like a scene to you? I wish you knew how much it hurts here," I said placing my palm against my chest.

"Now you feel the pain? When I waited for your call for hours and hours, I felt the same pain. I knew you were busy. I didn't ask you for the universe, but I deserved a star from that universe at least. I asked for an assurance that you were there. I wanted you to call, not for you to hear me out, but because I wanted to listen to your voice. When it crossed the limit, I couldn't care less."

"It is the third person who created misunderstandings. Believe me, I was working very hard to make you smile and to be able to stand next to you," I tried to convince her.

"It is too late now."

As I was on the ground, I saw two flashing headlights approaching the central ground at a speed which was above permissible limit. The headlights flashed right into my eyes. I saw a white sedan car that stopped with a drift and made a temporary sand squall out of the dust. The darkness and dust made it difficult to see, but I clearly heard the opening and slamming of the doors. As the dust settled down, three men approached us. The way those three had slammed the door, it was clear that they were in mood for some action.

"Can we help you Romeo?" The guy who stepped out from the driver's seat said in a heavy voice. He was still invisible as the headlights were too bright, blinding my vision.

"Sweetie," Noor said as she ran towards him. They hugged and that blew the remainder of hopes in my heart. They were about to kiss, but Noor was decent enough not to break me anymore. I stood up on my feet.

Danny came closer to me and I saw him for the first time. When Swati had described him as a strong man, she had forgotten to add very to the adjective. Danny was very strong, very muscular and very tall. All my fantasies of punching and bashing the bastard reversed in a moment and now I could imagine him doing the same to me. Plus, he had brought two of his accomplices who were equally strong; running away was not an option.

Seeing the chaos, the guard stepped out of the guard room and walked towards us.

"What is going on here?" he asked.

That guard had been the most hated person for me a few hours ago, but now he looked like a saviour. I thought he'd ask me to leave and I would peacefully leave the campus.

"Nothing uncle," one of the accomplices said. He took the guard aside and gave him some money and a packet of cigarettes. "You listen to your commentary."

The guard accepted the bribe and smiled. He left us there. I was shocked. I remembered Swati had also said that he was influential. Again she had forgotten to add very. The miscommunication between me and Swati was about to cost me my life.

Danny looked into my eyes and yelled. I closed my eyes in anticipation of danger.

"Uncle, can you raise the volume of the transistor," he yelled at the guard. "Bloody ruined my cricket match," he whispered slowly.

I estimated again how mad he was at me. One, because I came close to his monument claiming it to be mine, and two, for ruining his World Cup final.

The guard twisted the sound command to put the volume on full.

"Indians have been stressed all this while and a huge burden will be off their shoulders in about ten minutes," the commentary became loud and clear once again. It suggested the men in blue were close to the target, but I lagged far behind.

"We need to wrap this up in ten minutes. I have to watch the final over!" Danny shouted.

In that terror situation I managed to give volume to my voice.

"Can I talk to you for a minute?" I asked Noor.

"Talk to me," he grumped.

"I don't want to talk to you. I want Noor."

"I want Noor! You aren't scared of me, are you? You are challenging a lion in his own den!"

"Noor, can I?"

"Talk to me!" The lion roared for the first time. "You don't want to leave this campus on your feet?"

"I don't care how I leave this campus. Nor am I scared of you! Before you even touch me, let me make it clear that you have already wounded me. A part of me is already dead because of you.

So please let me talk to Noor. Please, I request you," I said joining my hands.

"Finish it man, we have to watch the final," the accomplice standing closest to the transistor said.

"Sweetie let me talk to him for a minute." Noor intervened and took me close to his car. The three strong men walked towards the transistor. One of them lit cigarettes for all three of them.

"Please leave the campus. He is very protective about me. He already hates you. Don't give him another reason."

"Strange! I am about to be beaten and you are showing concern. It seems like only he hates me."

"Please stop this. He is very dangerous you don't know him."

"He cannot hate me more than I hate him. He took the most precious thing I had. What did you see in him? What? What does he have that I don't?" I charged at Noor. For the first time in the evening, I saw guilt in her eyes.

"Tell me what is special about him?" I yelled again. She was taking a step back every time I charged at her. She stepped back till she hit the car.

"Oh the car," I said. "He has the car and that is what you always wanted. Dammit! That is what you wanted." I yelled as I punched the car. This time I was louder than Ravi Shastri and the lion heard me. I was too close to his monument. He stomped towards me.

"Sweetie, stop!" Noor yelled to stop him.

"I guess you got the answer, Nandu. It is not about the car or the muscles. It is the love and care that he shows for me," she said as she shrunk herself in his arms. "I never said it before, but I love you Danny." She turned towards him and kissed him on his lips.

That was the final nail on the coffin. I stood shocked and closed my eyes. I breathed heavily and it felt like someone had squeezed my heart inside my chest. The pain was unbearable. I clutched my hair with both my hands and made a squealing sound. I wanted to run away from there, but was too shocked to take any action.

Noor released her lips from his. "I will go inside the hostel. Take care."

She entered inside the hostel gate. Danny was totally blown away by the kiss. The kiss drained away his anger and he stood smiling.

The two sidekicks came to congratulate him. One of them announced, "Noor said teach him a lesson so that he never tries to contact her."

"She said that?" the lion confirmed.

Both of them nodded yes.

"This man cannot let me enjoy the moment!" Danny grumbled.

Noor exhibited a cruelty that I had never imagined. So many blows in one night made me lose all my senses. I laughed maniacally. I laughed louder and louder.

The laughter was annoying for the Romeo who had just got his dream kiss. He punched me in my belly to stop the annoying laughter. The punch tore my stomach, but I didn't stop. I laughed and laughed. Next, he elbowed my back to pitch me on the ground. But the laughter continued. He grabbed the collar of the gifted blue shirt and dragged me on the ground. The laughter continued. His sidekicks started to kick me where they could. The laughter continued. I was not feeling any pain because no pain could be worse than seeing your beloved kiss someone else. My voice lowered. The two sidekicks lifted me and made me kneel down on the ground. They grabbed me with the arm. Meanwhile, Danny opened the trunk of his car and pulled out a cricket bat.

With eyes barely open, I saw him coming towards me with a cricket willow. My laughter ceased and there was absolute silence once again.

The lion gripped the bat and stood a few feet away from me. He took his stance and aimed at me. He patted the willow on the ground twice and as the crowd cheered from the transistor, he used his muscular power to swing the bat towards me.

"Dhoni finishes off in style. A magnificent strike into the crowd. India lifts the World Cup after twenty-eight years…"

♦

"Nice men finish last," my friend whispered softly into my ears. I opened my eyes in the hospital, totally confused and perplexed. I had no clue why I was there. It took me some time to remember.

"You will be discharged in two hours," the doctor said to me, patting my shoulder.

I regained my senses. All I remember was a cricket bat loaded with rage approaching my face.

"Nice men finish last," my friend whispered again.

"Why do you keep saying that?" I asked my friend Satbir Kumar, famously known as Sattu. His name didn't match his personality. He was a tall, good-looking guy from Haryana. He carried a charm in his smile which was an attraction for girls. He was a friend who was more like my mentor for all the wrong things – a friend who was an ambassador of anti-relationships, a friend who made sure every brain around him was as corrupt as his, a friend who never wanted me to be nice.

"Because I warned you before," Sattu yelled, grabbing my shirt that still had blood stains. "Nothing good ever happened to a nice man. A nice man either ends up in a hospital bed or a mental asylum."

"This is not the right time for this discussion." A harsh voice interrupted the conversation, the origin of which was Keshav Yadav aka Keshu, the most mature member of our group. He was a tall, thin guy with a thick voice. He was the only son of his parents after five daughters. Although tall, his shoulders drooped under the burden of responsibilities.

"Let us go back to the hostel," suggested a high-pitched voice, generated by the vocal cords of Shardul Pandit. He was the runt of our gang, the shortest in height and with an equally broad, hairy body and very unnoticeable personality. But one thing that stood him away from others was his readiness to help.

After a short series of rumpus dissension and the doctor's clean chit, we got back to our hostel – the Eklavya Halls – the boys' hostel for dental students of ITS Dental College located in Ghaziabad. It was the place that had united the four of us for the past three years. In the vast campus, it was just a small building; but for us, it was our home. We were now in our fourth year of dentistry. Another two years and we'd be dental surgeons.

The nice man all my friends were talking about was me – Shiva Nandan Sharma, aka Nandu. I owe this ancient name to the mythological beliefs of my mother. She named me after the divine god so that I can have 24/7 protection from the almighty. The occult notion has worked for me for many years, but eventually it capsized. I lived the worst phase of my life. My girlfriend broke up a five-year-old relationship with me for a not-so-nice guy. The catastrophic event shattered me emotionally and the not-so-nice guy battered me physically. The bleeding nose and stitched forehead had well received the warning but the already wounded heart was stubborn and was not ready to give up. It desired Noor or nothing.

As a result, days were spent in silence and nights crying. I no longer mingled with my best friends. They were all worried, but no one talked about it. They tried to drag me to stupid parties and movies. I refused every time. I attended classes and visited the dental OPD, but with zero interaction with the outer world. To the world, I had forgotten Noor, because I didn't talk about her. But deep inside my heart, there was a storm, regret for letting her go and an obscure desire to be with her again. I kept all these thoughts to myself.

I still hang out with three of my friends. Keshu was my roommate. Hiding tears from him was inevitable. We shared our balcony with the neighbours – Sattu and Shardul. This shared balcony connection made us great friends. Another commonality between us four was our middle-class status. In the hostel full of the high-class brats, it was only us four who didn't match up to their standards. We didn't use expensive stuff like them. We didn't watch Hollywood movies like them. And the way we spoke English was understood by only us four, while the others mocked us for our vernacular accent. We were counted amongst the bright students of the class, whereas Keshu was famed amongst the top rankers. We were happy in our own world. All four of us had different views on different things, yet we respected the differences. That is what made our bond special.

Our hangout place was the small storage room on the terrace. The room was always locked, but being the sincere class topper, Keshu was trusted and given the keys by the hostel warden. Although honestly, we misused this power once in a while. We used the main door keys to sneak out for our late night movies and to attend uninvited weddings. This small room on the terrace was named the suggestion box. It was a square room where all four of us sat in our respective corners and brainstormed on various issues. We discussed life, relationships, careers and sometimes sex. The walls of the suggestion box were witness to many brutal arguments and various intellectual ideas. We had sneaked in an electric kettle into that room and during exam time, tea was made and the syllabus discussed inside this magical chamber.

After my break up, I avoided entry to suggestion box as it reminded me of my long conversations with Noor. The walls had witnessed the cheesy conversations between her and me; they had also witnessed the tears that I had shed.

Time passed by and with every coming day, I struggled to overcome the heartbreak without any help from external sources. Soon the final exams of the final year knocked on the door and I got a chance to finally deviate my mind from the stupid heartbreak.

We wrote our final exams, the successful completion of which would confirm a berth in a one-year internship at the college's Dental Hospital. As per the rules, after the last exam, we had to vacate the hostel. On the last day, for the purpose of celebration, we all met in the suggestion box to bid a final goodbye. For a change, the tea was replaced by alcohol. The buckets loaded with vodka and whisky were brought as a festivity.

We, as regular members, took our respective corners with the transparent glasses in our hands. Though the milestone was similar for four of us, the purpose of consuming alcohol was different for everyone. Keshu had worked his ass off during the past few months and before going into a hibernation of relief, he wanted to get drunk. Shardul had bribed god to help him during the exams and in turn, had stayed away from alcohol for three months. He wanted to end his three-month hiatus of conditional dryness. Sattu wanted to drink so that he could make a drunken call to some random chick whose identity he kept hidden from us. And me, who had been a teetotaller till now, was coerced to drink by these three. They wanted this miraculous tonic to heal my internal wounds.

Soon the transparency of the glasses was dominated by a dark looking branded ethanol.

"It smells terrible!" I shouted in disgust as I brought the glass close to my nostrils.

"Close your nostrils and drink it," Sattu suggested.

I squeezed my nose and took the first sip. I gave them the disgusted look again.

"Drink!" All three of them ordered in chorus.

The wounds were deep. The pain was unbearable. Peer pressure was high. I was forced to give away my alcohol virginity.

As the first drop of the miraculous liquid passed my food pipe, words came out of my voice box in a stammered voice.

It all began with, "I love you all. You are my brothers. You all mean a lot to me."

Few drops later, I described how the four years with them had been.

Few more millilitres later, I boasted of my virtual superpowers.

A glass dunk later, I was the best dancer of the city.

Few more glasses later, I wanted to buy the Taj Mahal.

And when my bloodstream was loaded with the internal wound healing tonic, I started to cry for Noor. I sobbed like a baby. All three of them gave up their corners and came to hug me. I cried continuously. I narrated my already known unsuccessful love story to the three of them. I did it on repeat. The first few times it sounded cute to them, but soon the repeat mode bugged them.

After handling three glasses, I felt an urge to destroy this earth. I was convinced that with my virtual superpowers, I could easily do that. But before doing that, I wanted to make one last call to Noor. I slipped my phone out of my pocket. The three of them acted like the Rapid Action Force to confiscate my cell phone. I was adamant to make the call. The rapid action force warned me not to.

I cried. I cried even more. After two hours of crying and narrating the same love story seventy-six times, Sattu lost his temper.

"Shut up!" Sattu screamed at the top of his voice.

There was pin drop silence in the suggestion box.

"I will destroy you if you take that name one more time." Sattu broke the silence showing me a punch. "Listen to me and listen carefully."

I sat on my corner, listening to him like an obedient child.

"Answer one simple question. Why can't you forget her?"

"I cannot. I feel like I cannot smile now. She took all the happiness I had. It is so hard to breathe without her…"

"Oh shut up!" Sattu screamed once again. "She was a goddamn woman, not your lung that you cannot breathe. Don't play a Bollywood cliché in front of me. She was just a chapter of your life. You read it and it is finished. Doesn't matter how good the book is, you cannot keep reading it over and over again. You have to close the book and move on to a new one."

Shardul clapped at Sattu's analogy. Sattu was a player and had coined numerous illogical theories and irrelevant statistics about dating girls. These theories were elaborately presented as and when the context demanded. He used attractive one-liners to endorse these theories and make them believable. Usually, they brought disgust to Keshu and me, but to Shardul, they meant something. He admired Sattu for his brilliant work in the field of flirting. He applauded almost everything Sattu said that night.

I was for the first time influenced by Sattu too. He made me realize how beautiful the world was and Noor wasn't the only one. The garden was full of beautiful flowers. All I needed to do was explore. All he wanted me to do was stop being nice.

"The first golden rule – never exchange hearts. Switch off the feelings and focus on the body. Love is just a polite euphemism for hormonal needs. The one who fulfilled your needs is now gone. You need to find some other body to feed these starving hormones. I know for a hard-core romantic like you, it will be difficult, but I will provide you with the mandatory assistance. All my life now onwards will be dedicated to showing you the path to enlightenment."

Sattu made many solemn vows that night. I knew that I was his next project, the target of which was ruining the nice man within me.

"Love is a disease and a kiss is a remedy," he announced towards the end of the night.

I was put to bed, but his words had made a deep impact. I had suffered enough with the disease called love. I needed a remedy.

Two Good Reasons

"Look at that… Just look at that!" said Sattu, pointing towards the screen of a laptop.

"I told you I am not interested in any of these," I replied in disgust. "I just broke up with the most perfect girl on this planet. Let me cry in peace."

"Friends don't let friends cry over a break-up. They help them overcome it," Sattu said.

"I don't want to move on. There is no way I can."

"Where there is a breast, there is a way. And where there are two, there definitely is a highway," Sattu stood up and turned the screen towards me.

"Look at them," Sattu continued. "They are too beautiful, too majestic, too innocent, too lovable…"

"And too many," intervened Keshu in between. "At least show him a single pair of breasts. Don't start with an orgy."

"No my friend, the first step in the healing process is to bombard his brain with too many breasts. For the last five years, he has been around only two breasts. His mind and sensations are jammed with a thought that they have only one shape, one kind, and one size. He has to know that this gift to mankind comes in all shapes and sizes – round, oval, hemispherical, circular, dome, hexagonal, saggy, intact, asymmetrical, and many others."

"Are those all shapes of breasts?" I asked.

"See he is showing interest. Sattu's therapy is working," Shardul whispered in Keshu's ear.

"Yes, these are the shapes which are available in a variety of kinds and sizes," Sattu said.

"Sizes like 32 B, 36 C…" Shardul replied.

"Don't misguide with semi-information," Sattu intervened, pointing a finger at Shardul. "Those all are the sizes used by the bra companies to sell their products. If you go by those terminologies, you can never think beyond the linen covering those majestic beauties. That linen is the biggest barrier between you and your path to salvation."

"Sorry," Shardul apologized. "Please enlighten us with the new terminologies."

"To understand breasts, you have to broaden the horizon of your thoughts. Size ranges from mammoth, huge, big, medium, small, extra small, yet to grow, coming soon, might not come to nipples only. These sizes are further classified into various kinds such as untouched, newly erupted, old but worth touching, new but not worth touching, overly touched, too big to be grasped with one hand, too small to waste one hand, etc."

"Oh my god! I didn't know that there are so many varieties available," I said with my eyes wide open.

"I would like to correct you once again, my friend," Sattu said, raising his index finger and wiggling it to show his disagreement. "These are not the available varieties. These are just varieties. You have to work hard to make them available to yourself."

"These things won't help me anymore," I said.

"You called them things," Sattu raised his voice. "Show some respect. From the prehistoric times, these have been the source of rejuvenation for the male soul, a cradle for the renovation of a broken heart and a source of mental peace. In short, it is the most acceptable and scientifically proven remedy for a break-up."

"I don't need a remedy. She broke up with me. I loved her when she loved me and I love her now when she does not love me. My love for her won't change," I growled.

"What you lost were not the last breasts of the world," Sattu said.

"You think my love was based on breasts? There is another organ behind this fascination of yours and that is called a heart. I loved that heart. My love was spiritual." I said, raising a question for Sattu, "Have you ever tried to feel a heart, Sattu?"

"I have. Believe me. I have tried thousands of times to find a heart. History is witness that whenever I've attempted to find a heart, my eyes found a cleavage in the process. And that cleavage is a slippery gateway which slides you into a totally different world. It is like you have dinner on the table but dessert is right in front. Naturally, any sensible man will pick dessert over the rest of dinner."

"I have no clue what you are talking about. Your theories are of no use to me," I said, scratching my scalp.

"Whatever happens, happens for the best. Maybe that break-up was for the best," Shardul said patting my shoulder.

"And after a break-up, whatever happens, happens for the breast," Sattu said.

"Give me one good reason why should I move on?" I said, still scratching my scalp.

"I will give you two – breasts," said Sattu, adjusting the laptop screen. "You will have to relax and just look at that."

The three of them left the room and the three naked women on the laptop screen took over.

I was not convinced by Sattu's short presentation over moving on. But this definitely laid the foundation for my first step into the mesmerizing world of breasts. From there onwards, whatever happened, happened for the breasts.

Meanwhile, we successfully passed our final exams and became interns. Sattu found an apartment for us at the Delhi-UP border. The reason was to enjoy the life of Delhi at the price of UP. Everyone agreed to his plan. The apartment was located in the youth society where the majority of residents were students of our age. Sattu picked the corner-most three BHK apartment numbered C-29. The usual rent for this big an apartment in such a locality was beyond the collective budget of four middle-class boys, but the apartment was believed to be inauspicious, so we got the occupancy at a very nominal rent. People believed everyone who lived in that house went bankrupt. Some conventional vaastu experts said the front door of the apartment faced some unconventional direction. No one wanted to live there. We made full use of people's superstitions. Overly religious Shardul hesitated, but Sattu convinced him to join us. The location was perfect and spacious to live our bachelor life. It was a few meters away from a restaurant named Chana Chabena Dhaba. This resto-bar soon became our hangout place. To give this ghetto a better reputation, we abbreviated it to CCD.

While Sattu, Shardul and I were focussing on having a relaxed life inside our new home, Keshu was preparing for his post-graduation entrance exams and decided to not be part of our awesome bachelor life. He got seriously committed to his long-time girlfriend Ankita and became more focussed on his career. Most of his time was spent in studying for the exams, so he was allotted an individual room. I took the smallest room and Sattu and Shardul decided to be roommates again. The living room was the common hangout place and a big forty-inch LED television was installed to watch India play cricket. Second-hand couches were brought to rest our butts while enjoying beer.

Sattu was very excited to move in to a new place and was managing everything to make our lives better. To add to luxury, he brought his father's old car into the garage. It was an antique white Maruti 800. Antique and rusted; rusted and loud; loud and annoying. But it served the purpose and that's all we wanted. It allowed us late night outings. It allowed us to execute the randomly made outing plans. It was our multipurpose adventure car. Once ignited, the engine was loud enough to wake anyone sleeping in a one-kilometer radius. On the contrary, the horns were on mute. Other defects included the headlights which were bright enough only to see a few centimeters ahead, the seats that were ripped off and missed springs and the windshield that had a few cracks. Overall, the maximum speed achieved without any visible or audible artifact was close to sixty kilometers per hour. Anything above that made a horrible sound like an asthmatic rhinoceros mating. Investing any money in the makeover of the car would have been a waste as it was like a dying old man on a ventilator. But this sick old metallic chunk proved to be a faithful companion and never let us down.

The new innings began at C-29 and Sattu took charge of our lives. Shardul and I were his two students whom he was training with his experience. Shardul had been his disciple for four years now, but had no success to his credit, owing to his quality of chickening out in front of girls. By now, the mentor had lost all hopes of training him. As a result, Sattu's entire focus was on me. He wanted to transfer his woman-hunting skills to me. He wanted me to be happy. He wanted me to overcome my heartbreak with another girl being the medicine.

I took his teachings seriously for I wished to smile once again. I wanted to rise once again. I wanted to live once again.

Net Practice

Sattu had been teaching me theory for over a month now. According to him, I was a fast learner and it was finally time for me to enter the practical world. He also wanted net practice for me before the major tournament. I bought his advice and started with it.

Sattu picked Devika Paranjpe, a famous wannabe of NCR and one of Sattu's ex-flings. He set me up with her on the phone. He gave me notes on what to speak and when to speak. Under his guidance, I was able to flirt with her. Finally, the day arrived when I was supposed to meet Devika.

The phone rang. The screen displayed 'Net practice calling'.

"Pick up the phone and put it on loudspeaker," Sattu whispered.

"Why are you whispering, I haven't yet picked the phone?" I said as I took hold of my cellphone.

"Whatever," he said clearing his throat. "Do as I say."

And I did as he said. I pressed the receive button and then the loudspeaker icon. With all caution, I put the cellphone on the coffee table and sat across Sattu.

"Come on, we are going out," Devika shouted on the phone, "No one is home. The car is all mine."

I was overwhelmed with the offer and before I could stumble, Sattu wrote the instructions for me.

"Tell her why are we going out, when no one is home?" I read exactly what was written by Sattu.

"Tell her? Tell whom?" Devika questioned.

"Idiot," Sattu whispered as he scratched out 'tell her' from the paper.

"I mean, why are we going out when no one is home?" I rephrased my question.

"Really, you want to come over?" Devika said.

"Why not?"

"Get ready then. I will pick you up in half an hour and then we will come to my place."

Before I could react to her invitation, Sattu scribbled a big 'OK' on the piece of paper. I resisted saying okay. Sattu showed a punch and after a few awkward seconds of silence, I said okay.

The call ended and the celebrations started. Sattu whistled and Keshu and Shardul lifted me up on their shoulders.

"Good job, my friend," Shardul said.

"What a catch man! She is driving all the way to pick you up. I hereby declare you the luckiest man on earth. You are getting the lady without spending a single penny," Sattu said as he hugged me tightly.

"Who said I am not spending a penny? I will buy a gift for her," I said.

"Why will you do that? Do you love her? Do you like her? Do you have any affection towards her? If the answer to all these questions is no, then there is no point in getting a gift. Make a note my friend, gifts and kisses on the forehead are very dangerous elements in the world of flirting."

"I am going to her place for the first time. It will be awkward going without a gift. It sounds cheap."

"The priceless gift she wants from you tonight is hanging between your legs," Sattu said as he pointed his finger towards my male organ.

We all laughed and I decided to go cheap.

I took a quick shower and as I came out of the bathroom in my towel, all three of them surrounded me.

"Use this perfume. This will definitely make an impression," Shardul said.

"Wear this shirt. It looks good on you," Keshu suggested passing me his shirt.

In the next two minutes, I received more advice than I ever had.

"Whoa whoa whoa… I am not going to war, neither am I going to bring the world cup home. Stop making it a big deal."

"It is no less than lifting the world cup, my friend. Even though she will lift your trophy, but it will give you a feeling of a victory."

"Thank you for all your valuable advice, but you are making me nervous. It is my first date. I have only talked to her on the phone. I will be nervous in the first place. I don't even know whether she will get a chance to touch the trophy."

"Do not talk like a loser! You have been chosen to gift her pleasure. Being your mentor, I have worked hard for you. If your thing doesn't go hard tonight, my hard work would be in vain."

"Stop training him and let him improvise," Keshu came to my rescue and set me free from my overly enthusiastic mentor.

Grabbing the wishes and ignoring the unwanted advice, I left from my place.

Downstairs, a red car was waiting for me. Devika waved at me from inside and opened the door for me. She gave me a hug as I sat beside her.

"She is way prettier than what Sattu described," I talked to myself. "Wait! Sattu never described her. He only described her lady lumps. Sorry, my bad! How can he even look at the lady lumps of this beautiful girl?"

We both locked our eyes and smiled for around two minutes. I remembered my mentor's advice – the first two minutes are to scan her body. But she is bloody so beautiful, how can I take my eyes away from her face? The curvy eyeliner over her eyes was the center of attraction. Her nose had a pink nose pin that was shining every time a car's headlight flashed on it. Her smile was catchy too. She tilted her head once or twice, probably to untuck her hair, and tapped her fingers continuously on the steering wheel. She was probably waiting for me to speak. How could I speak? I was lost in her eyes. I could not follow my mentor's orders. I only wondered why Sattu didn't notice this beauty. What did he see in her lady lumps? With that question, I moved my eyes to where he wanted me to at first place.

"Look at that, just look at that," I said to myself, surprisingly. Those are beautiful. The topography of her chest answered all my questions. Soon the center of attraction changed. She wore a pink shirt. The shirt was so tight that the top three buttons were struggling hard to keep themselves in the buttonholes. She probably wore it on purpose to make her chest look prominent. The tensed buttons provided a window to what was the most beautiful site at the moment. It seemed like the two beautiful lumps were staring at me through the window. I was staring at them with equal intensity. The figure-hugging top was suffocating them and they were crying for help. Every time I stared at them, they stared back at me, seeking my help to release them.

The Superman within me replied to them, "I will soon rescue you guys from here."

During my scanning, I forgot the owner of those lumps. Devika cleared her throat. The situation was awkward, but she smiled. I regained my senses and asked her to drive. She drew the seat belt and the beautiful twins were separated by an obliquely sliding strap. The strap also acted as a curtain for the window. The show was temporarily over for me.

She put on some music and drove on. With every third song playing on the radio she shouted, "Oh my god! This is my favorite song."

As she was driving, I pretended to focus on the road, but the truth was that my peripherals were still trying to catch a glimpse of the beauty. After a long game of hide and seek we reached her home and she sneaked me into her apartment.

We sat on the couch in her living room. She offered me water and some snacks. I gulped water, but said no to snacks. I saved my appetite for the dessert that was making me drool since the last few hours.

After a handful of stupid jokes and some utterly untuneful conversation, I got a chance to sit beside her. We looked into each other's eyes. I didn't want to waste any time, but she had all the time in the world to spare.

"I don't know what you will think…this is the first time we are meeting and it's in my house," she said looking into my eyes.

"I will think that you have a beautiful house, daddy earns really good money," I said, trying to be humorous.

"I really like your eyes," she said, exceeding the chain of compliments that I had initiated.

"I really like your shirt," I said, falsely appreciating what was the only fence between me and my dessert.

"I don't know what I should say now…" she said, confused.

Once I complimented her shirt, my brain started to plan how to approach. There was a moment of silence. Only the two brains were conversing with each other.

"How should I open the shirt? Shall I go for the buttons or directly slip it over her neck?" I said to myself.

"Will it be too early if we kiss?" her brain questioned her.

"I should go with one button at a time." I once again said to myself.

"I don't want to sound too desperate. Will he think I am desperate if we kiss?" she questioned her brain yet again.

"One, two, three… total nine buttons. If I open them at a speed of one button per three seconds, it will be done in twenty-seven seconds. That's too much time. I have to improve my speed."

"I don't even know what he thinks of me."

"Wait, I think I should kiss her first. A kiss will give a good start," I said the last thing to myself.

Shutting off the outflow of silent questions from an overly concerned brain, we came closer to each other. She kissed my lips really hard.

I was about to get lost in the kiss, but going per plan, I ripped off her shirt, releasing the tension of the top three buttons.

"My new shirt!" she shouted, showing concern for her shirt that got sacrificed while protecting her assets.

Before the ripped shirt could worry her, I slipped my hands on her back to rescue the twins from the cage. Though it was the moment of freedom for them, I was more contented than them.

My mentor had trained me right. He wanted me to make him proud and I did. His remedy was working. There was a smile on my face and for the first time, my past didn't stop me from achieving happiness. The first module of my training was complete. I succeeded in the net practice and that made me eligible for the next level.

The Championship

Minutely visualizing my breathtaking performance in the practice sessions, my mentor was proud of me. His teachings paid off and the smile on my face testified all else.

"Look at that smile," Sattu said, tickling me on my chin. "Now you know what you were missing."

"Yes I know, but I feel sorry now. I haven't replied to Devika's texts since that night."

"Don't even try to respond. That was just another chapter, and you read it. Move on to the next one," Sattu instructed.

"But that is unfair to her. She might be waiting."

"Here comes the nice man," Sattu taunted. "She knows why you were there. She wanted that too. Don't be too nice now. The frequency of messaging will reduce gradually."

"But I liked what happened that night. I want to do it again," I expressed my urge.

"That was only a practice session. Big tournaments are waiting for you. She was the easiest target even an average Joe can achieve. You have to achieve something big. Don't get boob blocked."

"What is a boob block?"

"It is a provisional but perilous state, yet to be recognized by American Medical Association. Symptoms include frequent craving of one set of boobs and inability to focus on other surrounding ones. Etiology trifecta – affection, emotion and slash or stupidity. Prognosis: very bad, and treatment: perpetual guidance by Dr Sattu."

There came another made up pathological terminology from Sattu. He could compile his own dictionary of made-up medical conditions.

"Where am I supposed to find them?" I asked, without raising a finger on his belief.

"Take off the emotional spectacles and open your eyes. All around you, boobs are looking for a guy like you with equal desperation. All you have to do is explore them with your discovery skills."

There was something about Sattu's tone. He enjoyed the taste of control. And to assure this control, he used his charming personality and various other methods. The firmness in his tone was enough to inspire anyone. Drawing inspiration from his words and confidence from my practice, I moved on to my new target – Sheenam Bajaj.

She was the girl who was deemed unachievable by the male community of the dental college. She never dated anyone. She never talked to any guy on campus. All we had heard about her were the rumors, source to which was credited to her attitude towards boys.

I interacted with Sheenam and somehow managed to get her phone number. I sent her a funny, cheesy message to initiate my move and she replied to it with emoticons.

"You will get your balls kicked," Sattu warned me as he saw me messaging Sheenam.

"It is a planned move. Nothing can go wrong," I said.

"I have been trying to get her since the last four years. I am working on it till date, and I haven't even reached an inch closer on my progress chart."

"Don't worry about that. I have been trying since the last four hours, and I have made remarkable progress," I replied with a smile.

"You already started? Without my help?" Sattu asked raising his voice.

"How did you do that?" Shardul asked the same question with the same decibel.

"Don't shout, you guys. I am losing my concentration. She is replying really fast. I have to catch up," I said.

"You are fitting into shoes too big for your size," Sattu said as he pointed his index finger towards me. That index finger had a veiled warning which I ignored. I was busy replying to Sheenam's rapid fire questions. I could see my act hurting my mentor's ego, but I ignored that as well.

"When you get kicked by her, feel free to come to me. I will get an ice pack for your balls." Sattu offered sarcastically. "I don't think I need your help anymore," I said to him as I showed him my cellphone screen which flashed a kissing emoji sent by the target.

Those flashing kisses brought surprise to both Sattu and Shardul. The latter appreciated my efforts, while Sattu left the room.

Conversation with her was funny and interesting. In two days, we were talking like we were best friends. Inside the campus, I was on the news as I became the only guy who talks to Sheenam. A scowl was visible on Sattu's face and was directly proportional to the number of messages swapped between me and Sheenam. I missed no opportunity to give him blue balls. I sat on the couch in the common territory to boast about my achievement. After every fifteen minutes or so, I sang the TV commercial jingle from the nineties – 'Humara Bajaj' to make it worse for him. It became the victory song for me.

Fed up of the message tones and my repetitive victory song, Sattu lost his cool and snapped at me. "Can you stop this nonsense? You won't get anywhere with this. You need some more coaching. From the easiest target, you skipped to the toughest. Easy there, Superman! Take one step at a time."

"I can smell jealousy. Are you jealous that I am about to get what you have been eyeing since the last four years?"

"First of all, I am not jealous, and second of all, you are not going to ride Bajaj. She is just playing with you and I am concerned for your reputation."

"Weren't the kissing smileys enough?"

"You are challenging my glorious experience with that dumb tiny yellow pouting smiley? I am the most bankable player of the sport you just learned to play. Don't run so fast that you fall with your face down."

"Thank you for your concern," I said without caring too much.

"I have been the best for the last four years in college."

"Maybe… because I wasn't participating."

"You are participating now. Prove it."

"You were the best, but still couldn't ride Bajaj. I think riding Bajaj itself will prove that I am the new best."

My narcissist comment loaded with pride and arrogance was followed by a big round of applause by Shardul. "Very well said. I think if you can get what he couldn't, that will automatically prove who the winner is."

"Riding is a far cry; if you can even kiss Bajaj, I will give away the crown to you," Sattu announced.

As the two of them were looking at me to accept the challenge, my phone beeped again. I checked the message and jumped in the air to announce what was written in the message.

"I want the house by myself tomorrow. Sheenam Bajaj wants to see me in private." I winked as I accepted the challenge.

"Let us see if that actually happens," Sattu yelled as he left the living room. His voice lost its firmness. It seemed like he was scared of losing his crown for the first time in four years.

Shardul gave me a hi-five and offered his help throughout this challenge.

Sheenam Bajaj was undoubtedly a tough catch, but Sattu forgot that I had been trained by the best. The charm worked and after exchanging around two thousand something messages topped by flirtatious emoticons, she was in my room. The reason I was able to achieve this elusive target was my honesty. I made one thing clear. There won't be any emotional entanglement.. And she not only agreed to that, but also thanked god. She had told me, everyone who had approached her was madly in love with her, and she was looking for a love-free casual relation. Her search was over with my honesty.

She came to my room the next day, looking stunning in a green kurti and red salwar.

"How do I look?" she asked.

"Like a red chilli," I replied with a sizzling sound effect.

She took that as a compliment and smiled. I didn't get why she was dressed so ethnic for a not so ethnic event. She told me opening a salwar is easier, one just needs to know the right knots.

"Allow me," I said as I moved closer to her. She raised both her hands to allow me to play with the knot. I raised her short kurti and got hold of the knot. The first attempt went in vain. My mighty hands failed to get hold of the miniature knots.

"You have to be man enough to know the right knots," she said criticizing my effort.

That hurt the feelings of the wild dog within me. I palmed her petite waist and pulled her towards me with my left hand. Grabbing her firmly with my left hand, I slid the right hand on her navel to get hold of the knots. Resting my hand, I allowed my index finger to enter the loop and flicked it away. Gravity was at its best and the salwar kissed the floor in no time. I pushed her on the bed to scan her legs.

"That was very manly," she said as she tried to slide her kurti downwards to cover her legs.

"Don't even try. I have won it and I deserve it."

I then jumped on her. She looked hurt, but enjoyed my manliness. She took off my shirt and commented on my underdeveloped pectoral muscles. "You need some workout."

"Do you think I care about these muscles? The muscle of your interest is very well developed."

She laughed and urged me to show it.

"You have to win it," I said.

She pushed me on the bed and jumped on me. If a petite girl like her could push me that far, that meant I really needed workout.

She kissed my unworked chest and moved down south to feel the only developed muscle of my body. She struggled hard to pull down my pants, and her hard work was welcomed by a trophy.

"It is hard already. I thought you have good control."

"It is not hard. It is paying a standing ovation to your efforts."

She laughed and felt the trophy, appreciating the muscles.

"I think it needs some more workout. I will be your instructor," she said as she grasped it with her petite hands.

"Be a good instructor and don't go tough on him. He has feelings too."

"Let me ask him what he wants."

'Humara Bajaj' was 'mera Bajaj' for that one day. I had fulfilled the challenge thrown by Sattu.

The next day was supposed to be my crowning ceremony, but Sattu, the man who was overly obsessed with this invisible crown, refused to hand it over to me. He called my act as beginner's luck and demanded another valid championship.

"Now that we both are equally skilled, let us reset the scores and count the number of kills we have by the end of the internship," Sattu suggested raising his beer pint in anticipation of cheers.

"End of the internship? That is ten months from now. Don't you think it is a long wait?" I said denying him the bottle bump.

"Yes, that is a long wait, but what you won was just one game. Play the whole tournament to win the crown. This glory is worth the wait."

He raised his beer pint towards me again.

"Done!" I said accepting the challenge and bumped my bottle to his.

"That is so awesome. Can I be a referee?" Shardul said raising his pint towards ours. "I will keep the track record of your scores. I will maintain a journal with the name of the target, date, time and your views about the session. I will name it 'The Dirty Journal'."

Sattu and I looked at each other. We gave it a thought and agreed to Shardul's idea. Shardul's father was a crime reporter in a local newspaper in Agra. He always admired his father for the kind of job he does. This gave him an opportunity to follow his father's footsteps, except that instead of crime, he had to report something equally unethical.

This tournament provided me with new opportunities to live my life. I drew inspiration from the tournament and confidence from my previous experiences to move forward. During my training process, I was taught some ground rules by Sattu. Some rules that Sattu followed while flirting.

Rule #1: The target girl should fulfill Angelica's criteria.

Angelica Vyas was a girl in Sattu's high school. None of us had ever met or seen her, but we had heard many stories of Sattu and Angelica. He used to boast about her beauty, body to be particular. Angelica's criteria meant that a girl to be hit upon should possess a body proportionate to that of Angelica Vyas. Sattu usually decided that by creeping up to the girls and estimating their stats and calculating the scores.

Rule #2: You are not allowed to hit on a girl your friend has eyes on.

I had already violated rule #2 by hitting on Sheenam Bajaj. I didn't care about the rules, and that made me a potential threat to Sattu's crown.

Ignoring the rules, I made the next move. I started with the girls who had showed interest in me in the last few years. I had been a loyal boyfriend back then, so I had ignored all these distractions. But now these distractions proved to be a great help in shooting my score. I attacked almost everyone – my classmates, my juniors, my seniors and also girls from the paramedical college. Age wasn't a bar for me. In about a month, I brought quite a few girls to our apartment. Shardul was kept busy making notes in his journal. He was more than happy for my success. Sattu was striving hard to get his form back, while Keshu was disappointed by the speed I was going.

I had shown the way out to another random chick while Shardul came to interview me for his dirty journal entry.

"Dude, wasn't she the big tit bimbo from the paramedical college?" Shardul asked curiously.

"She indeed was," I said as I gulped water from the bottle.

"Awesome man. She is a heartbreaker," he said as he opened the diary.

"Not for me."

"Tell me how tough it was to get her into bed and what struggles did you go through?"

"Getting her phone number was the biggest challenge, but once I got that, it was a cake walk."

"No struggles at all?" Shardul chuckled.

"Only one... It was hard to focus on her eyes with those jugs in the way." We laughed so hard that Keshu was forced to come out of his room.

"You are disgusting Nandu. I never expected this from you," Keshu shouted.

"Are you feeling jealous?" I said.

"More than jealous, I am ashamed," Keshu replied.

"Ashamed of my achievements?" I asked.

"Ashamed of you. I know you better than any of these. You always respected girls. And now look what you have become. You have mutated into Sattu. In fact, you have become worse than him."

"I appreciate your concern, Mr Know-it-all. But right now, I am in the middle of my journal entry. I will get back to you later." I ignored Keshu as I was flying high with my success.

"I fear later will be too late. I moved here to be with my friend Nandu — the gentleman Nandu. The one who respected girls, the one…"

"Sorry, but that friend of yours is dead. And can't you see how happy I am? No one likes a nice man. They like this man who lies to sleep with them. I respected them and what did I get in return? Just humiliation and harassment."

"Don't expect good deeds to bring results so soon. It is a long term investment. Don't stop being nice just because one girl couldn't see that goodness."

I stood placidly for a bit. He reminded me of Noor. I was in tears once again.

"You are scratching an old wound. I prefer we talk about it tomorrow," I said, hiding my eyes from him.

"I doubt if there will be a tomorrow. I am leaving this apartment right now."

I wasn't surprised by his decision. Like he knew me better than others, I too knew him in and out. He was stubborn and once he had made his mind, he stuck to it.

"You are overreacting Keshu. Please don't do that," Shardul said.

There was no point of convincing him. He was disgusted by my act. But I was too blinded by my success and too selfish to make him stop. One had to leave, and Keshu volunteered. Shardul tried to convince him. I didn't even attempt once. I locked myself in my room and kept thinking what had gone wrong with my perfect life. I could have never imagined that my happiness would come at such a big price. I lost my best friend.

Keshu left and gave us some bitter memories. He stopped talking to me. A four-year-old bond was broken. We paused our game for a few days, but was tough not to think about the trophy.

When things were at its worst, Sattu came up with an idea. He planned to convert Keshu's room into our playroom. He made some profligate investments and brought a cozy double bed and fancy lighting to decorate the recently vacated room. It became the most luxurious section of our apartment. We named it the honeymoon suite. Stag entry was barred in the suite. No one was allowed to sleep there unless it was with a girl. Sattu added a new rule to the championship. From there onwards, to be counted as a valid score, a girl has to be brought to the suite. Outside scores were always questionable as there was no alibi to testify them. As per Sattu, the suite would allow us to raise our standards, and we could target the high-profile spoilt girls now.

I agreed to his luxurious idea for other reasons. I didn't discriminate between any girls or any boobs. I liked all kinds and all shapes. That's why I didn't follow any of his dating rules. I agreed to his concept of the honeymoon suite because I could not wait to sleep in that cozy bed.

He also added a new prize to the championship winner. Apart from the invisible trophy that he claimed to possess, the winner would also get the permanent possession of honeymoon suite. That was the real motivation for me to win. The room had only one password to enter, and that was boobs. Sattu ensured that room provided all the luxuries possible as he anticipated he would overly use the suite. The windows were covered to ensure privacy. The room was painted blue to create an ambience. A king sized bed was brought into the room with a memory foam mattress. A drawer was installed beside the bed, full of protective latex from various manufacturers and in various flavors. A mini refrigerator too found space in the room which was loaded with cans of beer and bottles of vodka. The room was the epitome of luxury.

After sleeping in that bed for two nights, I realized I didn't miss Keshu anymore. I patted my back in self-appreciation for not stopping after he left. I had reached a phase when any time I was sad or tensed, I made a move. Bringing girls over became like a drug to me. It distracted me from my worries and struck me with euphoria as well. I needed it every time I felt miserable. It was a drug to which I got addicted, and there was no coming back.

30 Plus 1

"More than thirty!" Sattu screamed banging his hand on the coffee table.

"Thirty you said, I clearly remember," Shardul politely replied.

"No no no! I said more than thirty," Sattu said banging his fist on the table each time he said 'no'.

"Thirty thirty thirty! You said thirty." Shardul imitated Sattu by slamming his fist every time he said 'thirty'.

I had no clue what was going on in the living room. I was in the honeymoon suite, busy wrapping up things with Polly Mendosa.

Well, Polly was just another random girl for me. I barely remember anything but her name, and another characteristic. I will reveal the other characteristic soon. I had to figure out the root cause of the squabble that was going on the between two.

The night after Sattu challenged me, I started scoring girls with a variety of pick-up lines. My friends thought I would soon mutate into Sattu, but there was a difference. He had a few ground rules. I, on the other hand, had no rules. Also, I was not selfish like him. I never turned down help when someone approached me as their wingman. Shardul was aware of this kindness. We all went to our favorite nightclub RPM. Almost every second Saturday was spent at RPM. And almost all the times, I scored one or two.

"How does he do that?" Shardul asked as he saw me making out with a girl.

"He is just a mad man. He lies to them, and lies a lot," Sattu replied with a pinch of jealousy.

"Whatever he does, he is too good at it. He might defeat you in the championship. You need to start working on that."

"It is easy to score at a nightclub. The crown belongs to the one who gets the girl into the honeymoon suite. Right now, I am leading the count."

"You are leading right now, but the way he is progressing, I don't think you can hold on to the crown for a long time."

"No chance! He can never be me."

"True that! He can never be you because he is not selfish. He cares about me."

"What do you mean by that? Now you want to tell me that you are changing your wingman. You want to make him your mentor?"

"I didn't mean that, but now that you brought this up, I might give it a second thought."

"You son of a bitch, I got you phone numbers of a dozen beautiful girls. If he gets you even two, you change my name to whatever you want."

"You only get me numbers, and that doesn't do any good to me. He's got me more than that. A hug three weeks ago, a peck on the cheek last week and if we progress with the same speed, I might get lucky in two weeks or so."

"Keep dreaming and do inform me the day your junk gets lucky."

"Don't be so jealous. I know you trained him, but his execution of your teachings might get him the crown."

"Over my dead body! Or shall I say on my atrophied dick which is impossible, because this dick's appetite is more than the hair on your body."

"Why do you have to use my hair as a landmark?" Shardul said. He was always made fun of because of his hairy body.

"Because whenever you open your mouth, you spill nothing but idiocy."

"This ain't idiocy. He will soon defeat you, and you will be devoid of that invisible glory of yours."

"First of all, it is not invisible, and second, I am not going to lose it. Do you want to bet on it? Let us bet."

In the loud music and flashing lights, Shardul once again darted his eyes on the couch I was making out on. He noticed my progress, and that boosted his confidence.

"Let us bet," Shardul said confidently.

"Brave boy! Come on, give me a number," Sattu said as he pulled out his wallet from his back pocket. "How many girls will you think he will score by the last day of our internship? By scoring I don't mean his over the couch making out…it has to be in our honeymoon suite."

"What is his score till now?"

"Forget that. Reset button pressed. The battle will begin from tomorrow. The bet will be a secret between the two of us. It will be different from the championship."

"Deal," Shardul said as he shook hands with his jealous wingman. Correction… jealous ex-wingman!

"Since it is all about boobs, I say if Nandu can show the suite thirty boobs till graduation, I will give you two thousand bucks," Sattu said.

"Two thousand is a big amount. And thirty even bigger. Can you reduce both of them?" Shardul was a little hesitant.

"What happened to your confidence now? He still has nine months till graduation. And if you start saving two hundred and fifty rupees from your stipend every month, you will be able to pay me the money," Sattu chuckled. "Shall we seal the deal?"

"Thirty girls is a big number, bro."

"Idiot, I said thirty boobs, which anatomically measured comes up to fifteen girls," Sattu said as he tapped Shardul's naïve brain.

"Oh, thirty boobs!"

Confused Shardul once again stared on the couch. This time, he saw me lying flat a hundred and eighty degrees with some random girl.

"Yes!" he shouted.

It seemed like his confidence level was inversely proportional to my reclining. The more I reclined on the girl; the more inclined was his confidence.

"Deal – two thousand rupees for thirty boobs."

The agreement was verbally signed. I didn't know anything about this, but I was the one they were betting on.

I joined the conversation late, but none of them told me about the bet.

"How do you do that man?" Shardul said as he palmed my back with appreciation.

"All thanks to my mentor," I credited Sattu for my performance.

Sattu didn't show any signs of appreciation. He was busy sipping his whisky.

"Why don't you get our friend something?" Sattu said pointing towards Shardul.

He knew how difficult it was to get Shardul laid, and he wanted to prove who was a better wingman.

"Alright, let us do it." I accepted the challenge. "Any particular set of boobs you wish to grope, Shardul?"

"Asking a homeless man if he wants a bungalow or an apartment?" Shardul said, his sarcasm reflected his helplessness.

"My homeless friend, your days of vagrancy are finally over. Tonight I am going to find you a shelter," I said as I rubbed both my hands.

"Don't make his dreams float on cloud nine. Just get him something. The shelter is not what he desires; a foundation stone will be enough for him," Sattu said.

"Have faith in your wingman buddy. Not only the foundation stone will be laid, but your iron pillar that only has your fingerprints until date will be raised too." I used a goofy metaphor to raise his hopes further.

"Please do that. I am tired of taking the matter into my own hand. I want to give it to someone else's hand," Shardul said, mocking a cry.

"Can you guys tell me where can I find more beer?" A random girl asked as she approached us with a wobbly gait. She looked sloshed. With her slurred voice she couldn't make herself clear.

"Beer anyone?" she shouted again.

Shardul had a beer bottle in his hands. He was about to offer her the bottle. I stopped him midway.

"Actually, ma'am you can find beer behind that door," I said redirecting her to an isolated corner of the club.

"Thanks," she said and left.

"Why did you do that? I was about to offer her my beer. She could have become my friend!" Shardul yelled.

"Come out of that friendzone, you idiot. She has more to offer." I said as I snatched the bottle from his hands.

"What are you doing now?" Shardul asked.

I pulled his belt and poured the beer inside his underwear.

"Are you mad!!!" Shardul screamed, loud enough to grab the bouncer's attention. "That was the most expensive beer."

"Ssshhhh! Don't scream…you will thank me later for this."

I grabbed his hand and followed the same beer craving girl.

"Wait here," I said, instructing him to stay in the dark corner.

"I went to the girl alone. She was drunk enough to hardly understand anything. I still managed to bring her with me.

"Right here," I said pointing at Shardul.

"Where? I cannot see anything," she stated in a drunken tone.

"Let me open it for you," I said as I pulled Shardul's zip.

"What are you doing?" Shardul whispered in my ears.

"I told you, stay quiet and don't move, and when I wink, you will stick your pillar out of your underwear. And the movement has to be robotic," I whispered back to him.

"Right here," I said pointing at his groin area.

I winked and like an obedient student, he did what I asked him to do. He simulated a precise robotic movement to stick the pillar out.

"You said unlimited for hundred rupees," she said.

"A hundred rupees and you can stick to that till tomorrow," I replied with confidence.

Shardul had no clue what the conversation was about. He stood unmoved with his pillar hanging still from his body.

The drunken girl slipped a hundred rupee note towards me and kneeled down. As per Shardul's desire, she took the matter into her hands. She did more than that. She sucked the matter, erasing all the fingerprints. Shardul was on cloud nine. He moaned like a girl. His eyes secreted pleasure and that was the authentication that I had succeeded as a wingman.

I left that dark corner, and we waited for Shardul in the car.

A few minutes later, Shardul joined us dancing and singing. His joy was immeasurable, and his confusion was a hundred times immeasurable.

He kissed me and hugged me.

"How did you do that? A girl paid you a hundred rupees to blow me. I didn't know I was that popular."

"Easy there, Superman!" I said as I drove the car.

"The girl paid to get laid?" Sattu said, surprised. "What kind of deal is that?"

"You are welcome guys," I said raising my collars.

"Please tell us what kind of exchange offer was that," Sattu asked curiously.

"Every night at a club is the first ever drinking night for at least one girl. She was that first-time drunk and therefore beyond sloshed. These kinds of girls are brought here by their experienced friends who totally forget about them once they are drunk. She was drunk and lost all her friends. She was craving for more beer and approached us. Thanks to our black shirts that made us look like bartenders. I just played with her sloshed brain. I told her there is a beer tap in that dark corner, and then later her confused brain forced her to believe Shardul's junk to be a beer tap and hence she was sucking on it."

"What the fuck! Is that why you poured beer in my pants?" Shardul said.

"I told you; you will thank me later."

♦

After that incident, Shardul became more confident about the bet and sanguinely raised the bet money to five thousand rupees. He gave a chance to Sattu to withdraw, but impudent Sattu stuck to it.

That brings us to the early morning of graduation day…

Shardul sat on the dining table with a piece of paper. Sattu joined him with a glass of water.

"Here we go, my ex-wingman. Twenty-eight boobs till last night and he is with Polly inside," Shardul announced as he added a '+2' on the piece of paper.

"Thirty boobs till graduation. Not bad eh," Sattu said as he looked into the piece of paper. "I wish he had time to fondle with one more boob. You would have won the bet."

"I *have* won the bet. Thirty fresh and different boobs till graduation, which is today."

"The bet was if he scores *more* than thirty, I will lose five thousand rupees to you."

"You said if he scores thirty, I will win five thousand rupees. Here is the complete list. All thirty are different."

"*More than thirty!*" Sattu screamed banging his hand on the dining table.

"Thirty you said, I clearly remember," Shardul politely replied.

"No no no! I said more than thirty," Sattu said banging his fist on the table each time he said 'no'.

"Thirty thirty thirty! You said thirty," Shardul imitated Sattu by slamming his fist every time he said 'thirty'.

As both of them argued, I escorted Polly to the main door.

"What are they fighting about?" Polly asked inquisitively.

"I have no clue. I will see what the matter is," I said as I walked her out of the main door. "I will see you tonight at the graduation ceremony."

Before I could ask them what they were fighting over, Sattu shot me with a question.

"Hey, I have a question. It is a bit personal, but why does this Polly push her bra now and then."

"That is not personal," I said as I pulled the juice out of the refrigerator. "That is very personal, so shut up!"

"I have seen her doing that too," Shardul added. "Seriously dude, you need to tell us."

"Keep it to you," I said as I sat beside them.

"Yes, we promise." They both said.

"Polymastia," I said.

"We are not asking her full name," Sattu said. "We are asking why she keeps pushing her bra."

"Polymastia is not her full name, you idiots. It is the reason she keeps doing that," I said.

"What the hell is polymastia?" Sattu asked.

"It is a condition where a female has an additional breast. Polly has polymastia. With the conventional two-cupped bras, it is uncomfortable to adjust that third boob and hence, she keeps pushing her bra."

"Wow. Additional breast! Is it uncomfortable for you too?" Shardul asked.

"Not at all, it is like buy two get one free. It gives you more choices to play with," I replied.

"Every time you are with her, it must be like a threesome," Sattu said, and they both chuckled.

"That is it. I don't want any more jokes on Polly," I said as I got up from my chair.

"Her name being Polly is itself a joke," Sattu said and they both laughed.

"Grow up guys. I have to get some sleep before getting ready for the night," I said as I left the living room.

"He is damn lucky. He scored three boobs in one night," Sattu said.

"Hang on!" Shardul shouted as he pulled out the paper again. "That shoots the total to thirty plus one. That makes it more than thirty."

Sattu looked at the paper appalled. He knew he had lost the bet. Even his diabolical trick didn't do any good for him. Polly's polymastia made Shardul a clear winner.

"Damn you, Polly!" Sattu screamed.

Graduation

The mega event of graduation night arrived. Few were excited, and few were nostalgic. Some were shedding tears, some were swapping stories, and some didn't give a damn. They were enjoying the free booze in the cocktail party hosted by the dental college. Everyone was excited to see their names prefixed with 'Dr'. Sattu and I were excited to know the result of our championship. Technically the counting was done and the designated referee Shardul knew the winner, but my eyes were looking all over the ground to score one last minute quickie.

Being the class representative, I had to give the obligatory farewell speech on behalf of all the batch-mates. I was well prepared, but the fact that three hundred people were attending the ceremony made me nervous. And what do I do when I am nervous? I turn to Sattu, the coolest person on campus. And what happens when I ask him for advice? I regret it.

His admonishment for my anxiety was two shots of tequila. Being the newly-corrupted member of his alcohol brigade, I didn't know the power of tequila. "Two shots are nothing. I can handle that," I said to myself, underestimating the power of tequila, ignoring the fact why this sour son of a gun is never consumed in a 250 ml glass.

Two shots down and I replenished the lost confidence. I tore the piece of paper that had the script of my speech. The female class rep was delivering her speech, and I was the next one. I asked Sattu for last minute motivation. He motivated me using his favorite topic – boobs.

"You are a boob bastard. Go and get squeezed. You can never lose. Go, knock them down!" Sattu yelled right into my ears.

Already intoxicated with tequila, I climbed the stage and took the podium. Tequila and boobs are a dangerous combination. The paper I had torn had been on my tips, till I reached the podium. I stood up and looked at the audience. All eyes were looking at me to speak the words of appreciation. Four big loudspeakers in each corner eagerly waiting to announce my speech. That shit load of expectation was enough to format the stored content in my brain vaguely. By the time I opened my mouth, I could only remember the salutation, "Good evening, Honorable Chief Guest, the Honorable Dean, my teachers, colleagues and loving juniors."

A long beat followed this. I had struggled hard to pretend I was sober. My head was spinning, but my feet were firm. When in trouble, as a force of habit, I located Sattu in the crowd. With his both hands he squeezed his chest and mouthed 'boob'. And the rest of my speech was history…

"We are all boobs," I roared. The intellectual heads in the front rows drooped down. I saw a few of them inserting their index fingers into their ears to confirm they had heard me right.

"You heard me right. We all are boobs. I remember when we entered the college, we all were baby boobs. The faculty and administration worked hard on us. They sucked us, licked us, and squeezed us to bring the best out of us. The administration kept us under strict covers to protect us from the outer world. They supported us and held us together, which made us disciplined. With every growing year, we grew firm and today, we are standing strong, disciplined and skillful enough to attract the world. We are perky, we are juicy, and today the time has come that we all unhook ourselves and release ourselves to showcase our talent."

I didn't realize what I was saying, but the speech sure did make some impact on my classmates. They wooed in support. By the end of my speech, I banged the podium with my fist.

"It is time to release ourselves. It is time to shake and show the world we are the best creation of god. We have the power to make everything happen. We have the power to convert every 'no' into a 'yes'."

The speech was motivational enough to make all the graduates stand up and throw their graduation hats in the air. Teachers and parents, on the other hand, were disgusted by my speech, but the drunk and tipsy graduates surely had fun. They applauded and whistled for me. I was being appreciated for something I had never planned. I was suddenly the hero of the class. Everyone came to congratulate me, except the ones who had come with their parents. I was yet to realize where it went wrong.

After taking our Hippocrates oaths, receiving our degrees and greeting every classmate, I received a text message from Shardul.

Come to the suggestion box right now.

I looked around to see where Sattu was. He was missing in the action. I ended my meaningless social conversations with my classmates and walked towards the hostel. I entered the suggestion box and saw all three of my friends. I was surprised to see Keshu after several months. That was the first time I saw him since he had moved out of our apartment.

"Hey!" I waved at him, and it was very awkward.

It was Shardul's plan to make us meet which he executed very well. To end the awkwardness, he decided to announce the results of the championship.

"As we know, two of our players are sweating hard since last one year to win the prestigious crown. Tonight is the judgement night," Shardul said as he opened the dirty journal.

"Wow! It has been one year. Time flies," Sattu said as he moved towards me to shake hands.

But Keshu's presence in the room made me uncomfortable. I was trying my best to avoid eye contact with him.

"The winner of the crown is…" Shardul took a pause, looked at all of us and shouted the name out, "Dr Nandu."

I jumped in the air out of joy. I was excited to win the championship and crowned as the new Love Guru. Sattu, on the other hand, looked annoyed. He shouted "Fuck you!" and threw his glass on the floor. I was probably too excited in the celebration to realize when he left the suggestion box. Shardul was the only one who congratulated me. He didn't reveal the score, but he thanked me for getting him closest to a girl. He also urged me to mentor him.

After a congratulatory dialogue between me and Shardul, he left the suggestion box, leaving me and Keshu behind. It seemed like a plan to allow me to sort out my differences with him. There was an awkward silence till Keshu came to me.

"Congratulations," Keshu said shaking hands with me. "You must be happy now?"

"Why not?" I said hugging him. "It was my debut. Winning the title on a debut is always good."

"Good for you."

"Are you happy for me?"

"Not really. What you won is a meaningless crown. What you lost is way more valuable. You lost almost everything you were proud of. Your friends, your dignity, your morals, your…"

"Stop it!" I said to interrupt him. "Why do you always see what I did to others? Why cannot you be on my side and comment on what Noor had done to me? She broke my heart when I was a good man. Now I am a jerk, and every girl wants me. That is the way it works. I didn't lose anything."

"She broke your heart and to fix that broken heart, you broke a hundred other hearts. Do you think that is fair? You lied, you cheated, and degraded to such a level that you take pride in calling yourself a jerk. You are living a shallow life. Destiny took away Noor, but you still had so much to cherish. Instead, you chose a different life and it robbed you of much more. You lost all your friends. It won't be too late when you are standing alone with your fake triumph. It is time you realize how expensive this remedy has been."

I was already drunk, and such words from a person who was so dear to me broke me down completely. I burst into tears. I fell on my bottom and rested my back in my corner.

"This isn't all, Nandu," Keshu continued. "Karma is much more powerful than we think. It will punch you back when you least expect. It is keeping the account of hearts you are breaking. I don't want to say that, but life works in a circle. You do good and good gets back to you. You do bad, and you will not be able to count your miseries."

I was not scared of karma; I was guilty of my actions. He left me alone in the suggestion box assuming I will come up with a solution. I sat there for hours and reflected on what he had just said. The darkness in that room made me realize my lies. The twelve months of sin flashbacked and projected on those four walls. I felt like punching the walls, but that wouldn't reverse what had been done. The happiness of becoming a dentist and winning the crown faded.

The championship was over, and so was my hangover. But the drug had clogged my veins. I was addicted to boobs. It was everywhere from my mind to my speech, and I had the constant urge to feel them. I had to change myself, which was challenging, especially being around Sattu. I took a step back and decided to retire from being a jerk. I wanted to be a nice guy again.

Kingdom of Boobs

College life was over and we were out in the real world. Keshu was the only one who knew what he wanted to do. Shardul had a faint idea. Sattu and I were totally oblivious.

"What will you do now?" I asked Sattu, who was reading the newspaper on the couch.

"I think I will take a shower," he answered as he tilted his head to smell his armpits.

"I meant what will you do now with your career?" I rephrased my question.

He smelt his armpits again. "I guess you got the answer."

"You cannot make a living out of sniffing your armpits."

"I won't do that to make a living, you dumbass. It was a metaphor to remind you not to ask such a dumb question in the morning."

I snatched the newspaper from his hands. "We need to be serious now."

"Good idea," he said, taking the newspaper again. He didn't give a damn.

The same year, our dental college's sister branch announced its academic expansion, and as a result, the top rankers were invited for an interview for the position of junior lecturer. As the majority of the top ten geeks were busy preparing for the post-graduation entrance exams, they passed the baton to the next ten students. Sattu and I fell in that category. Unfortunately, Shardul was rank 21 and he missed out on the interview call. Sattu and I got the interview calls, but the venue was our own college. I had to face the same panel who had witnessed my embarrassing farewell speech.

The interview panel was headed by the college dean and two other professors. Quite ashamed of my act, I entered the boardroom. They stared at me as I walked in, my eyes focussed on the tip of my Cherry Blossomed black shoes.

"Have a seat, Dr Shiva," the Dean commanded.

"Thank you, sir," I said as I raised my head for the first time.

"Can we see your resume?" the professor on the left asked.

My shaking hands took out my not-so-impressive resume. "Sure sir," I said.

"Who in this campus doesn't know you?" Dean said folding my resume. "After all, you have been a class rep for five years. You don't need a resume. Everyone knew you and those who didn't know you in those five years definitely know you after the graduation day."

"Fuck my life," I mouthed.

Dean chuckled. "We don't need to see your resume. We have squeezed you enough. You are a boob we can bet upon."

Surprisingly, all three experts sitting on the interview panel praised me for my daring act. They laughed hard and asked me to say the speech again. I could only recall a few parts of the speech.

Listening to the reconstruction of my epic speech, the Dean announced. "Congratulations. You got the job in our Greater Noida campus."

"Thank you, sir." I smiled and suddenly my heart beat went back to normal.

I got up from the chair and walked back to the door.

Sattu entered the boardroom after me and he came out jumping, indicating he had got the job too. We both were selected.

"Our first job!" he shouted in excitement.

Sattu was too happy to work as a lecturer in a college that had ninety percent female students. He looked forward to that as a land of opportunity. On the other hand, it was a testing time for me. At the time when I was determined to stay away from girls, this land of opportunity could prove to be fatal in my path of deaddiction.

"This is cool man. We will be working at the same place," Sattu said as he took the driver's seat in our antique Maruti 800.

"Yes, it is cool. But let me make one thing clear I am focussing on my career now. You won't distract me anymore," I said as I rolled the seat belt across my abdomen.

Sattu laughed so hard that his voice dominated the sound of the engine. That surely pissed me off and reminded me of the conversation between me and Keshu.

"Why are we friends with Sattu?" Keshu used to ask me all the time.

Sattu's corrupt mind and sharp tongue always caused contention between Keshu and him. Keshu had repeatedly questioned, and I had always convinced him to continue our friendship with Sattu. No matter how his tongue and mind were, his heart was unadulterated and his love for us had been pure.

For the first time, I agreed with Keshu's views on Sattu.

I felt like punching him. I folded my fist and cracked my knuckles to warn him. He knew what I was capable of doing and that brought an abrupt cessation to his laughter. He promised to take me and my words seriously.

We went shopping straight away. The joining date was in a week. We went to an expensive salon to get the best haircuts. It was an elite hair salon where the professionals were using technical terms like Mohawk and Fohawk. For us those terms were new, and as a repercussion of this miscommunication that followed, we ended up getting undesirable hairdos. Two hours of hassle and two hundred bucks later, we went to our regular barber and said, *"Bhai side se chote karde."* This one-liner did better communication than any other.

We wanted to look good for our new innings. We invested a lot on ourselves and why shouldn't we? We were going to invade a fortress full of female soldiers.

Before we commenced our professional life, our apartment suffered another loss. Depressed by joblessness, Shardul moved out of the apartment. We tried our best to make him stay and even volunteered to pay his rent for some time, but he refused any kind of favour. He moved back to his hometown Agra. Sattu saw this as an opportunity to expand his lustful endeavours.

On the day of joining, Sattu spent almost an hour in front of the mirror. "We have to nail this bro," Sattu said while giving a finishing touch to his tie knot.

"Don't you think we are slightly overdressed for this job?" I said looking at our ties and blazers.

"Don't you know what is at stake? That is a dominant female campus. Not only students, but the faculty is largely female as well. We are going to enter the kingdom of boobs. Big boobs, small boobs, large, extra-large; we will find all kinds there. Do you still think we are overdressed?"

"I still think we are."

"I don't want to take any chances, especially on the first day. Experts have said – the first impression is the last impression."

I dropped my blazer and decided to the keep tie. He drove us to the college in our antique car and to save us from chagrin of owning a century old car, we decided to park it in the parking lot closest to the exit gate which resulted in a good five hundred meters walk to reach the main building, which in turn led to sweaty bodies.

Excitedly, shedding away the gallons of sweat, we entered the kingdom of boobs which was supposedly meant to welcome us. We were waiting inside the office for the dean to assign us the departments. Sattu wanted us to be in the same department, but I was silently praying to god to land me in a different department than him. I was on the road to improvement and he was the biggest hurdle. I wanted to jump this hurdle without hurting the feelings of the hurdle.

"Congratulations," the dean said as she entered the room.

"She is hot too," Sattu whispered in my ears. I nudged him to keep his mouth shut.

"Look at you two gentlemen," she said as she sat on her revolving chair. She complimented us on our overly dressed attire.

"Thank you," we said.

"Your resume was impressive. Based on the details we would like to assign you the department of oral and maxillofacial surgery (OMFS)."

"For both of us?" I asked with my eyes plumped open.

"Yes, both of you. Our OMFS department has maximum patient attendance in a day. We need young doctors like you to help the senior staff share the load. Plus, it will be a good learning experience for you two."

She asked us to report to the Head of the Department. We left her office for the OMFS department.

Dentistry has nine major branches and each branch has a separate department in dental colleges. In this female dominated field, OMFS is the department that usually males opt for. It has blood, stitches, fractures, surgeries, wires and operation theaters.

On our way to the department, Sattu showed his anger.

"Why god why!!! There were nine departments and you threw me to the only boobless department. Why? What did I do wrong?"

Seeing him, I felt the urge to settle my scores with god too. I looked at heaven too and silently questioned god.

"Why god why? There were nine departments and you threw me with this boobmaniac. Why? What did I do wrong?"

We both were sad for two different reasons. Keeping our sadness confined to ourselves, we faked a smile before entering the bloody department of OMFS.

We anticipated to be welcomed by twelve boobs, but all we saw inside the staff room were six dicks sitting around a rectangular table. The reason why I called them dicks was because they were very rude to us. The center of the table was occupied by the HOD Dr Rastogi, who was the leader of the rude gang. We can call him the dickhead as he headed the rest of dicks.

The department had three professors, two associate professors and one senior lecturer. Being new and junior in the department, we were supposed to behave and obey the senior faculty.

We gave our introduction to the faculty. Dr Rastogi left his chair and offered it to Sattu.

"I guess you are appointed the new HOD," he said mocking Sattu as he was overly dressed in a blazer and tie. The rest of his team laughed at the joke.

Before being placarded by the staff, I pulled open the knot of my tie and folded it behind my back, stuffing it into my back pocket. This gave me an opportunity to laugh at him.

At the staff table, everyone seemed arrogant. They were lazy and over time had been spoilt by the sarcastic over smart dickhead Dr Rastogi. He liked to crack jokes, mostly sarcastic and mostly silly. Being the junior most staff, we had to laugh at them, mostly forcefully. He found pleasure in teasing people so he picked a few students every day, called them to the staff room and made fun of them over different reasons. He pointed their mistakes and overshadowed them with his knowledge. His act was backed by his team and this was their best time-pass. It was humiliating for the students and they were scared.

Sattu soon joined the humiliating team. He became a loyal team member and contributed to the sardonicism by picking on students as much as other staff. He couldn't see boobs inside the staff room, but once he saw the students, his smile came back. He didn't make any move for first two weeks. This was his research phase. He wanted to mark his territory so he picked all the beautiful girls, gathered their info and marked them as his. He made contacts in the admin office and the staff there helped him with all the required information. He wanted to rule this kingdom of boobs. As much as he liked dominating, he loved the challenges too. He invited me to join the battle to which I refused explicitly. I was focussing on the right things for the first time.

Apart from laughing at silly jokes, gossiping like girls and harassing the students, I was assigned duties to train the students in the clinic. Out of a group of fourteen students posted in the department, the junior lecturers were supposed to make two groups and lead one group to clinical training. Sattu picked the seven hottest girls for his clinical group and left the handful of males and not so attractive bunch for me. I didn't complain at all. I enjoyed teaching irrespective of gender and looks. I was the most sincere amongst our department faculty, therefore, the most liked by the students and disliked by the other faculty members. I didn't participate in their gossip and didn't force myself to laugh at their jokes. Neither did I waste my time during tea break, nor did I share my lunch with anyone. I was left out. That made me a saving grace for other students. They liked me and loved the way I taught them. Alternately, I was earning respect.

In the last five years of university, my brain had gone through thousands of pages of hundreds of books. It had explored numerous informative websites, dug down zillions of research papers, drilled down numerous teeth in a countless number of shapes, and tolerated tantrums of a girl who never understood my feelings. I had survived. But within two weeks of my stay in that department, my brain lamented for the first time. It showed the symptoms of wear and tear. It ached like someone was slamming it with a sledgehammer. I wasn't able to take that. My brain hated me as much as the other faculty members.

On the contrary, Sattu did everything to please them and was soon their favorite. He wanted me to be in their good books and sometimes invited me to outside department parties with them. I never attended them, for I had enough of them in six days of the week. Spending the remaining day of the week with them would mean more chances of a nervous breakdown. I used Sundays to rest my brain. I knew this was the real world and I had a hard time grappling with it.

An Encounter with Angel

It had been a month. Every single day I forced myself to love my job. Every single day I failed to do so. I was looking for excuses to stay. The maiden paycheque wasn't enough to tempt me to stay. From what my body was putting into that job, I deserved more than just the basic salary.

"One month in my department and you are still alive," Dr Rastogi commented sarcastically on my accomplishment. "At such a young age, you are teaching and guiding students. It must be a great feeling, right?"

"Damn it. I hate this place. I hate what I am doing here." My partially degenerated brain revolted, but I had no guts to bring that to my lips.

"Yes Sir, it is an incredible experience," I said, calming my thoughts and bluffing a big smile on my face.

"What is the most exciting part of your job?" Dr Rastogi continued.

"Lunch breaks. I only like lunch breaks." My poor brain revolted again, but my lips had something else to say.

"The surgeries, the lectures, sitting here and tutoring students – everything is so interesting. I wonder why we have lunch breaks.

They are such a waste of time," I said, yet again suppressing my views and faking yet another smile.

"I like your dedication. Keep it up. You will go very far one day," Dr Rastogi praised me.

"I want to go far far away from this department." I had another violent lull outbreak inside my brain.

"Thank you, sir," I said instead.

"Good afternoon, sir," Sattu said as he entered the staff room. "Can I steal Dr Nandu for a lunch break?"

"Yes, please. Take him with you and make sure he eats something. He is too dedicated towards work and doesn't like lunch breaks," Dr Rastogi said leaving his chair.

I left the department for the cafeteria.

"I hate this place," I grizzled while walking in the corridor.

"What happened?" Sattu asked.

"This place sucks. It is full of idiotic people. Teachers don't like to work. Students don't like to study. Everyone sits idle. I came here to learn and to teach. The only thing I am learning is how to fake smiles and control anger. The only thing I am teaching is ethics."

"Welcome to the real world bro," Sattu commented.

"I am quitting today."

"Don't do that. I am here for you. We have our fun time daily."

"I know we have our fun time daily but the departmental torture overrides that fun," I lamented.

"Who told you to quit the boob game and become a sage? We could have had lots of fun if we played another championship."

"I don't have the power to answer that question. Neither have I power to withstand that departmental agony. I have already written a resignation letter," I said pulling the resignation letter out.

"Bro, it's a big decision. Are you sure?"

"I am sure. I have to quit… quit… and quit!" I said raising my voice.

The voice was too loud to create an echo in the corridor. Sattu turned back to check who had heard my hatred speech. Luckily, there was no one.

Meanwhile, I noticed a silhouette approaching us. It wasn't clear whose silhouette that was. It was sure it was a female figure walking confidently towards us. The figure reached the distance of distinct vision and the suspense was broken.

Sattu was trying to calm me down while I had my eyes gazed at the female figure.

"Are you listening to what I am saying?" Sattu said.

"Of course, I am," I replied. The truth was that this was the last thing I heard from him. The moment the silhouette was disclosed and the mystery female figure appeared in front of me, I was lost. It seemed I was in the different world and Sattu was the background singer singing a romantic number from a romantic Bollywood movie.

My eyeballs got fixed on the mesmerizing beauty and the ear drums went numb as the brain entered the dream mode. The girl approaching us wore a black top and black jeans, waving her white doctor's apron in her forearms. The unauthorized catwalk generated the tapping sound from her shoes. While walking, she tried to tie her untangled hair with a clutch. She had a well-chiseled face with clear skin. Her broad red lower lip bounced as she walked in haste. Her forehead was spruced with a tiny black bindi. The ears were penta-pierced, and a different color earring passed through each piercing. As if this wasn't enough, a pinpoint mole on her neck made her more desirable. While I was busy scanning her beauty, she passed by. Her fragrance misted into the air, compelling me to inhale deeply.

The song paused for a second as she looked at me.

"Good afternoon sir," wished the diva.

The song resumed.

Her lovely voice created an echo in my eardrum. I closed my eyes to capture the moment in my brain. The moment left me bemused.

Before I could react to the sense-hijacking moment, Sattu snapped his fingers in front of my eyes to interrupt the dream. Throughout this episode, he was so busy convincing me not to quit that he had missed the diva passing by. He assumed that I was paying attention to his valuable words.

"Did you get my point?" Sattu said as he snapped his fingers again.

The babbling organs were brought to peace. The mesmerized senses were brought back to business. The thoughts that were bombarding my brain soon got converted into dreams.

"Yeah… yeah… oh yeah. I got the whole point. I got everything," I replied. By everything I meant the wonder that just passed by.

"Do you still want to quit?" Sattu asked.

"Nope! Not at all. I want to stay here now," I declared as I tore my resignation letter into several small pieces.

"You know what you want?" Sattu asked again.

"I know exactly what I want," I said as I tossed the pieces of paper into the air. I spread my arms and rotated 360 degrees on my right foot. I was filled with joy.

"I am so glad that my speech worked and you changed your mind," Sattu said taking credit.

Love Versus Lust

After finding a marvellous excuse to stick to my job, I felt happier than ever before. I sat in the department with a smile and explored the other departments in search of the mystery girl. I spent more time in the cafeteria than normal. Sattu liked the fact that I was cutting myself some slack and was socializing with other people. He didn't know the real reason behind that. He was busy wooing good looking female students. He brought a couple of them to his room and suddenly became famous amongst them for all the wrong reasons.

"Disgusting dude!" I yelled at him after seeing him escort one of our students out of our apartment. "She is your student. Respect that relation."

"Chill bro. In the medical profession, there is no relation like teacher and student. It is called a senior-junior relationship. Not that I am of her father's age. She is only four years younger to me," he said in his defence.

"But how do you face her in college after banging her at home?"

"Good question. That is why I avoid eye contact with her in my room. I go with doggy style."

"Ugh… Shut up!" I said in disgust.

"Forget that. Now that you are socializing at college I want to challenge you to another game.

Two months' salary at stake and the winner gets the suite back. I am sure you won't refuse if you see this one girl." Sattu pulled out Shardul's dirty journal and reopened it after a long hiatus.

"Wasn't I clear before? I am not playing any game and you better burn that journal," I said as I tried to snatch it from his hands.

"No dude. I will hold on to it forever," he said swaying it away from me.

"It has some darkest secrets. Throw it before it jeopardizes our image."

"No one is reading it apart from us. Out of any of us, you should be more proud of it. This is the saga of your conquest."

"Stop it. I don't want to go back to that."

"I opened this journal for one last time to throw a challenge to you. There is a new intern in college. She is so hot that once you see her, you are going to blow your mind. The task is that between you and me…who gets her to the apartment first. Her name is Tanishq Batra," he said writing her name on a new page.

I took the journal and pen from him and scratched the name from that page.

"Not a chance. Am I not clear enough?" I said.

"She is the hottest of all the girls. She is Sheenam Bajaj times two."

The offer was very tantalizing, but I was determined.

"I don't care. I am focussed on my career," I said resisting the temptation.

"Alright, as you wish. Don't be mad at me if you see her sleeping with me. Don't tell me I didn't give you an opportunity."

"I will not." I wanted this discussion to end.

The next day at college he took me to the department she was posted. We peeped into the department through the door.

"There she is." Sattu pointed at a girl wearing a mouth mask.

The moment she took her mask off, I was surprised. She was the same mystery girl! I kept staring at her. Sattu continued his commentary on her looks, but again, I entered my dream world. The same song played in my ear drums and my equilibrium was lost yet again. Before I could penetrate the outer layer of the real world and enter the virtual paradise, Sattu shook my hand.

The music faded and so did the smile on my face.

"Did you see her? Isn't she hot?" he said as lust drooled out of his mouth.

I got mad at him. He was drooling like a hungry dog that had not eaten a bone in years.

I got hold of his crotch and clawed his testicles with my right hand.

He screamed in pain and looked at me confused.

While grappling his valuable twin assets, I declared, "This beautiful girl deserves respect. She deserves true love. Keep your eyes away from her."

He pleaded to me to leave him and I did so once I was convinced he had got the message.

He scoffed and stretched his crotch to allow his groin to breathe.

"You could have killed me," he yelled.

"I will kill you if you look at her like that again and I am serious about it," I said, setting an admonition.

"What happened to you suddenly? I have never seen you so aggressive."

"I saw this girl before you and I don't know why I feel some sort of connection. I want you to stay away."

"So you are claiming copyright on her or do you mean to say you are in love?"

"Love… maybe."

He laughed and continued laughing for some time.

"You don't remember what this love did to you? You want to bang your head against the wall again?" he said as he pointed at the stitches I had received as a token of my failed relationship.

"Noor was the past and I was a kid back then. I am more mature now and I know what love is."

"You only know what being stupid is. You have evolved with great skills capable of tricking any girl into your room, but instead, you choose to love. Something is wrong with you."

Something was wrong with me. I had never felt like that before for anyone. The reason was the mystery girl – Tanishq. She was out of this world.

I apologized to Sattu to make peace. He forgave me but he said he would still go for her. He threw me a different kind of challenge.

Love versus lust.

Bad man versus nice man.

He will be the bad man and I will be the nice man. The challenge was interesting, but tough. I had never wooed a girl being a good guy, while he had an amazing track record of being a bad guy.

To accept his challenge, I had to convince myself that good guys are still desirable. I had to obliviate Sattu's theory of nice men finishing last. It was tough to do that as I had tasted success being the bad guy. But doesn't good always win in the end?

Trusting the godly messages scripted in various books, I accepted the challenge.

Helping him was his experience with girls, his popularity in college and his secret sources. His drooling tongue that candidly spilled lust all the time was against him.

Helping me was my belief in the good and my love for her. My body's cognitive uncooperativeness after seeing her was against me.

I wanted to win this challenge not only for Tanishq, but also to make Sattu a believer of good. The two-month salary was nothing against the promise I asked Sattu to make – if I won, he would stop being a bad guy and start respecting girls. If he won, I would have to give away the suite and also the attempt of being a good guy.

The next day we sat at the department and Sattu brought some useful information regarding her from his anonymous sources. Like a true sportsman, he shared it with me.

"She is a transfer intern here from some dental college in Pune. She moved to the city recently and her beauty is making news for all the good reasons. Apart from me and you, a handful of boys of this college also find her desirable. Competition is tough."

"Any idea when she will be posted in our department?" I asked Sattu.

"Not sure, but some sources say she aspires to be an oral surgeon, so she might be keenly interested in our department."

"Seriously?" I asked almost jumping out of my chair. "Are those sources reliable?"

"Don't ever doubt the credibility of my sources."

Our conversation was interrupted by the department peon.

"The HOD is calling you two to his office," the peon said leaving the two of us confused.

We went to see the HOD in his chamber.

"Boys have a seat," he ordered. "I have a favor to ask. There is a new transfer intern to our college. She has missed two weeks of her internship in our department. So I want one of you to tutor her personally for four days and cover for those two weeks. Train her in the minor OT and teach her everything."

Sattu and I looked at each other and hoped that he was talking about the same intern. The job was definitely tedious. One had to stay after college hours and sweat extra for no extra income. None of us would want to say yes. But if this new intern was Tanishq, this would give us a chance to be around her and anyone of us would die to do it.

"Which of you two will volunteer?" Dr Rastogi asked.

We both didn't say a word. It was a gamble.

"Come on you two," he asked again as he opened his register. "Her name is some Tani…"

"I will do it," both Sattu and I interrupted in unison before he could say the full name.

"Great, but I need any one of you?"

"I will do it," Sattu said raising his hand.

"I can do it too," I said raising my hand in the same manner.

"I have to pick one of you. Prove your brilliance and make my job easier." Dr Rastogi said.

"I will go first," Sattu said being restless. "I am a magnificent orator. I love to speak and I enjoy teaching students. I don't do anything after college so I don't mind staying a few extra hours. And last of all, I love students. I love to be around them."

Sattu was in the good books of the HOD and he was great at influencing people. I knew the HOD will prefer him to me, so I didn't even give a try to prove my brilliance. Sattu looked at me and winked. He knew he had won this battle.

"You enjoy teaching students and you love to speak! That is interesting," HOD said. "I give you the duty to lecture the year three students. Dr Shiva will take care of this intern."

His decision left me dumbstruck. It was the most unexpected statement. I looked at Sattu, and this time, I winked at him wickedly. I learnt another valuable lesson. Silence is gold.

The HOD asked me to leave while Sattu stayed back.

He told Sattu that he didn't like me much and that is why he had handed this tedious job to me. His lovable Sattu was given the easy task of lecturing the third years. Sattu learnt a lesson too. Sometimes being in the good books of bad people leads to bad things.

Excited about the new appointment as a personal tutor, I danced in the washroom for a couple of minutes.

I was supposed to be around the new intern in the minor operation theatre and work on patients there. No other student was allowed to enter the minor OT. I felt bad for the other students, but the fact that my mystery girl and I would be there all alone didn't let me mourn for long. I was busy orchestrating myself for the first impression in front of my angel.

Around Her

"You look good. Is there any special occasion?" the HOD asked me.

"Nothing as such… Beautiful sunny day," I replied hiding the truth.

The number of compliments I was getting that morning was a sum total of all the compliments I had received since I had lost my trademark child cuteness, which was in high school.

The occasion was Tanishq. I was supposed to spend the day with her. I wanted to leave no stone unturned in the preparation.

I shaved off the stubble and applied face pack to make my face glow and match her complexion.

I got a manicure done so that when I point at certain things while explaining, my nails and fingers looked good.

I got my shirt and trousers ironed by a professional dry cleaner and shoes polished by a cobbler.

And lastly, to make a mark of my aroma, I brought an expensive cologne and carried it in my bag and sprayed it after every half an hour.

I prepared myself well. Sattu witnessed my preparation and was surprised as he had never seen me spending so much time talking to my own reflection in the mirror.

I was waiting for Tanishq inside the department. She was late so I was sent with the patient to the minor OT.

"Get the patient ready and wait for the intern before doing any procedure," the HOD ordered.

I took the patient inside and waited for Tanishq. The patient was an old lady got cloyed over waiting past her appointment time. I had to calm her down by wearing the dentist's gadget.

After twenty minutes of my meaningless conversation with the old lady, Tanishq entered the room in a flash.

"Hello. I am sorry I got stuck in traffic. I am looking for Dr Shiva Nandan?" Tanishq said panting.

Apart from saying that one line in a blaze, she hustled many other words, probably the reason for getting late. I gawked at her with my mouth wide opened and feet tapping to the music set on by default every time my body witnessed her presence.

"Am I in the wrong room? I am looking for Dr Shiva Nandan, is he here?" she asked again, confused.

"Yes... No... I mean yes..." I stammered. I took a deep breath and rephrased, "No for the first part of your question and yes for the second. I am Dr Shiva Nandan."

"Don't pull my leg. Please tell me where Dr Shiva Nandan is?"

"I am not pulling your leg."

I was nervously answering her questions, probably that was one of the reasons she didn't take me seriously.

"I know I am new, but I have had my fair share of ragging. Let us be serious now. Where is Dr Shiva Nandan?"

"Right here," I said pointing towards myself.

"Shut up!" she screamed.

She dropped her bag and rolled her sleeves. With the look of a tigress, she moved towards me and grabbed me by my apron collar. This definitely was not good. She glowered at me and signalled to me to move aside. She grabbed the patient's OPD card and read all the required medical information. The old patient who showed signs of petulance moments ago, was now too scared to complain. She cooperated.

"Bring me the gloves and mouth mask," she commanded me.

One after another, she lorded. Like a scared cat, I followed all of them.

"Load the syringe with local anesthesia and pass it to me," she said gearing up with the dental accessories.

And then began the surgical procedure of extracting the wisdom tooth. She did everything by herself and I was her assistant. Being a teacher, I was monitoring the procedure. She made few mistakes, none of them too severe. I didn't have the nerve to point out those errors. I was enjoying being dominated by my student for the first time. Her dictatorship continued as she successfully uprooted the wisdom tooth.

"What drugs do you prescribe here?" she said as she took control over the OPD card.

"I can fill that for you," I said agitatedly.

She handed over the card and I filled all the details of the procedure and prescribed the drugs. Under teacher's signature, I wrote Dr Shiva Nandan in block letters. Then I handed over the card to her for her signature.

"Why is the card already signed?" she questioned. Then she looked at the signature, and seconds later towards me.

"I am really really sorry," she said. After that, she said sorry for around thirty more times, most of the time holding her ears. I couldn't help smiling.

I said smiling, "Why didn't you believe me when I told you I am Dr Shiva Nandan?"

"When I was told I have to see Dr Shiva Nandan, I thought he would be an old, grumpy, fat professor. I had an entirely different image in my mind. But when I saw someone so young and kind of dashing, I thought maybe you are one of the interns ragging me as per the tradition of this college."

"I know the name is a bit ancient," I said in my defense.

"Only a bit? My grandfather's name was Shiva Nandan too," said the patient who herself was close to eighty years old.

Her comment made us all laugh. The more Tanishq laughed, the more I kept falling for her. She held my left arm to maintain her balance.

The laughter made her cheeks red and her eyes wet. She finally ended it up with a deep breath and let go of my arm.

"I need some water," she said wiping off the joyous tears with her two thumbs.

"My name is Shiva, but unfortunately, I don't have river Ganga flowing through my hair," I said as I removed my head cap. The gel mixed with sweat made my hair all matted like that of Lord Shiva.

She laughed at the joke again. "I have never laughed so much in this college."

For the complete day, I made her laugh and she made me smile. I was guiding and mentoring her while working on patients. There was a significant waiting list of patients. And I didn't want to waste time on a lunch break. We skipped our lunch break. I convinced my body that it didn't need food because my heart needed medicine, which was her laughter.

After a few hours of fun and knowledge exchange session, she asked, "Aren't you hungry?"

"Yes I am, but first we need to clear this waiting list," I replied looking at the OPD cards.

"Dedication. I am impressed, Dr Shiva."

I blushed. When you are in love, you tend to speak to yourself a lot more than in normal situations, and the worst part is that a little boy sitting deep inside your brain replies to you. This response is usually absurd and misleading, but generates a big smile on your face, inevitable to hide.

"We are taking a break for five minutes. I brought my lunch and you are sharing it with me," she said taking all the OPD cards away from me.

I couldn't miss the chance of sharing food with her. I agreed. We sneaked out into the waiting room and she opened her lunch box.

"Matar paneer," I said excitedly.

"Yes," she replied wondering why I was so excited.

"That is my favorite." Before she could formally offer me a bite, I attacked the paratha that accompanied mattar paneer.

"That was delicious. You are an excellent cook," I complimented.

"Thank you, but do I look like I can cook?"

"You didn't cook this?"

"My mom did. I am more into eating."

"Say thanks to your mom."

"I will. I come from a foodie Punjabi family. We cannot live without food."

"Well, miss little Punjabi, isn't it with every human being? I don't think anyone can live without food," I said.

"Yes, but others eat to live; Punjabis live to eat," the proud Punjabi said as she wrapped up the lunch box.

We went back to the OT to treat the remaining patients. That day we wrapped up thirty minutes after the regular closing time. There was no one in college except the security guards and the two of us.

"It was a nice day." I said, locking the department door.

"Just nice? It was a wonderful day. I would say it was my best day at college so far," she said.

"Thank you. I look forward to beating the legacy of this day tomorrow."

We walked through the corridor towards the college entrance. She kept on sharing some fun moments of the day while I was busy questioning myself. "Should I ask for her phone number?" I got an ambiguous answer. 'Yes' said the heart and 'no' said the brain. During situations like these, our heart becomes optimistic while the brain sails in the boat of pessimism. Who to trust is a difficult choice to make. Confusion was big and the route to the main gate short. We reached the main gate and I handed over the keys to the security staff.

"Thank you once again, sir. Goodbye," she said and left. I couldn't ask for her phone number. But I couldn't complain about how the day had gone.

We followed the same routine the next day. She brought some more paneer in her lunch box and brought an extra paratha, especially for me. The laughter was an essential part of this day as well. But at the end, I couldn't ask for her phone number yet again.

In the three days, she finished her required hours and designated patient quota. She was more than happy, but I was sad that it all had come to an end. I could not ask for her phone number in three days, but had definitely made an impression on her. She respected me for my knowledge and the way I treated. She said she would like to become like me, which was the biggest compliment from any of my students.

I came back to my department and the HOD appreciated me for my hard work and selfless service to the department. Sattu knew it wasn't selfless, but he kept mum. He knew how happy I had been in the last three days.

"Lucky man! Did you ask for her phone number?" Sattu asked.

"I could not. I was too scared," I replied.

"Scared of what? If memory serves me right, weren't you the one who approached the most unachievable girls without any fear?"

"That was an entirely different case. I didn't have anything to lose back then. Now I have a lot to lose."

"What's the worst that can happen?"

"She is amazing. I haven't met someone like her. Not only is she beautiful, but she is so sweet from inside. She talks way too much. She laughs like a kid and gets angry like my mom. She has the courage to kick anybody's balls. She is simply adorable."

"Dude, I can see you are in love. Be careful, don't land yourself in trouble," Sattu warned.

"I know it is no less than love. Every time I look at the door, I feel like she will come from there, laughing and chatting," I said as I pointed towards the door that was behind my back.

"That is a serious condition."

"I know it feels like she is somewhere near. I can hear that laughter again."

"What the hell is that?" Sattu shouted looking towards the door. "There she is, laughing and chatting."

That is what happens when the universe works to make it happen. I stood up in shock too.

"Hello sir," she said with a smile. "I brought lunch for you. It's your favorite mattar paneer."

I was so moved. Sattu looked at me surprised. She was loud enough to attract some attention. The rest of the staff looked at me too.

"Excuse me," I said to the staff to end the awkwardness. I left with her to go to the cafeteria. We chatted for another half an hour.

The same day at home, Sattu talked to me about a serious issue. "I quit the challenge. You win. I saw in her eyes that she likes you."

"Does she?" I asked excitedly.

"Yes, brother. The nice man won. You were right."

"I cannot believe my ears," I said.

"Fortune favours true love. That is when the universe plays its tricks. That is why she was with you for those three days and you nailed it."

I wasn't still sure if Sattu was saying those words. Since the time I have met him, he had been an antonym of love. For the first time, he was endorsing true love. Not only that, he promised to lend his support to win Tanishq's heart. He had also accepted defeat. An avalanche of questions exploded in my brain and I shot all of them to him.

"It cannot be only because you saw love in her eyes. There has to be more to it?" I asked suspiciously.

"That is one of the reasons, but apart from that, I haven't seen you so happy in my life."

"What about when I was with Noor?"

"Not this happy."

"What about when I won the championship from you?"

"That was a fake happiness. You weren't happy with yourself."

He got me thinking again. Was this a sign of his maturity? Or was this because he had lost yet another game? His mature behaviour was also bringing suspicion. What if he wanted to use me as a guinea pig to see how Tanishq reacts when a teacher approaches her?

"Now that you have accepted defeat, will you change yourself? Will you start respecting girls?" I said.

"Who said that? I didn't accept defeat. I just said you won."

"Isn't that the same thing?"

"*Not at all!*" he screamed. "I didn't lose. I forfeit."

With that one word, all the suspicion was gone. He could not accept defeat.

"So what next?" I asked him.

"Here is all the required information that will help you." He handed over a piece of paper to me. It had all the information concerning Tanishq. Her birth date, address, enrollment number, marks in college, father's name, etc.

"That's creepy," I shouted without knowing the importance of that information. "Where did you get this from?"

"I got it from my sources at the admin office," he replied calmly.

"What do I do with this information?" I asked.

"Surprise her on her birthday," he said.

"That is in February and that's not anytime soon."

"Her address is there?"

"Yes. It says Green Park."

"Tomorrow you are going to Green Park."

"Why am I going to Green Park?"

"Because she drives to Green Park every day. Tomorrow after college, we will execute our plan. You will be getting a ride from her till Green Park. Keeping account of traffic, you will have approximately one hour to chat with her and know her."

I said yes to his brilliant plan. As part of my homework, I googled some random address in the Green Park area as my fake designated destination.

Next day after college, Sattu located her car – the white Maruti Swift Dezire – in the parking lot. He went to the library on the second floor from where he could keep an eye on the car as well as the main gate where I was waiting for Tanishq. I was supposed to pretend I was walking out of the main gate and not waiting there. He called and I picked up the phone.

"Alpha to Charlie. Alpha to Charlie," he said.

"Shut up and tell me if she is in the car yet," I said.

"Alpha to Charlie, her coordinates are 28.66 degrees north and 77.45 degrees east. She is approaching the car. Over."

Sattu never misses a chance to find excitement. He made this event look like a mission. I joined in to match his excitement.

"Charlie to Alpha, let me know when she drives towards the gate. Over."

"Alpha to Charlie, the car has begun to move towards the main gate. It will reach the destination in 0.0015 hours. Over."

"Stop it, you fool. How much is 0.0015 hours?" I asked ending the military conversations.

"In less than one minute."

I panicked as I was running out of time. I had to look confident while lying. Instead, I got nervous. I started walking towards the gate and encountered Chagan Lal, the only barrier between the gate and the road where I had to walk. He was the security guard to whom I have been so nice that he never misses a chance to strike a conversation. He was an old man in his late fifties. He was very sweet but spoke so slowly that before he finished one sentence, a snail could cross a road twice.

"Namashkaar doctor sahab," Chagan Lal greeted me, joining his hands.

"Namashkaar Chagan Lal Ji," I said as I continued to walk. I tried my best to ignore him.

"I am having a headache since morning. Can you write me some medicine?" he asked.

I wanted to ignore him, but the Hippocrates Oath came in between. I named him the best medicine ever invented for a headache.

"In fifteen seconds, you should be out of the main gate," Sattu ordered me on the phone.

I did my duty in front of Chagan Lal, but he didn't stop talking. I asked him to excuse me as I was on the phone, but he began to crib about his headache. He surely said that a headache was killing him but at that moment, I felt like killing him myself.

"Go outside the gate, you stupid fool," Sattu screamed as he started a countdown. "Five, four, three, two, one… Go now."

Before I could take any action, Chagan Lal began another story and I was obliged to pay attention to him. Tanishq drove by and I could only see her car from a distance. I felt like strangulating Chagan Lal's throat, so I gave him a tempestuous look.

"You dumbass. She left. Mission failed!" Sattu swore at the top of his voice and hung up.

I was left standing at the gate with Chagan Lal with a wish that I never knew him and an urge to punch him.

Then a miracle happened. The white Swift Dezire took a u-turn and came back to the main gate.

"Hi Tanishq," I greeted her as she got down from the car.

"Hi sir." She said and turned towards Chagan Lal. "Sorry, Chagan Uncle I forgot to give you these medicines. You told me in the morning that you have a headache. I brought you medicines. Take one now and one after your dinner."

She arranged for a water bottle and made sure he took his medicine in front of her. In a few minutes, Chagan Lal was smiling. The old man put his hand over Tanishq's head and said, *"Jeete raho beta."*

I felt contrite for my act. I wanted to strangulate that man. How could I be so selfish? At the same time, I saw Tanishq earning those blessings which she truly deserved. Her empathy for the old man showed how caring she was. There was a storm of mixed emotions. I didn't know what to say, so I stood still, watching them talk. She showed more compassion than I ever showed to anyone. She listened to him with all the patience and asked him about his daughters. After the sweet exchange of words between them, she turned towards me. "Sorry sir, I totally forgot you were here."

"I was better forgotten. I don't deserve a girl like you," I said to myself.

"Sir?" she snapped her fingers to grab my attention. "How come you are here?"

"Sir has to go to Delhi," Chagan Lal answered on my behalf.

"Where in Delhi?" she asked.

"Green Park," I replied.

"Come with me. I will give you a ride. I am going to the same area."

"Are you sure?"

"Absolutely. Come, have a seat," she said moving towards her car.

"Thanks."

Chagan Lal said goodbye to both of us.

I sat in her car and the ride began. It started with her asking me a few obvious questions like why I am going to Green Park and if I knew anyone there. I answered them exactly the way Sattu had taught me. She started to chirp in her usual style. I was so touched by her act of kindness that I decided to speak my heart out in front of her.

I imagined hundreds of Sattus sitting on my shoulder and cheering me, "Go for it!"

I heard those three syllables more than twenty times when I finally decided to say it. Before I could spill the first word, she entered the highway and her foot dropped on the accelerator. The car was flying on the highway. It forced me to hold the side rail of the door and recheck my safety belt. I asked her to slow down but she said that is was the usual for her. I wobbled on the passenger seat as she ruled the driver's seat. That fear erased all the courage that I had gathered a few minutes ago. The brain that was cooking proposal thoughts entered emergency mode and was looking into the body's emergency combat manual. My lips that planned to spill love were now reciting the *Hanuman Chalisa*. One by one, all the fictitious Sattus dropped from my shoulder.

She safely dropped me to the destination in less than forty-five minutes. I named her the daredevil. First I thanked God for saving my life and then I looked for a washroom to piss away my fear. I told Sattu that I couldn't talk to her much as I was busy saving my life. He was mad at me, but promised to come up with some other plan.

Trip to Heaven

"You are going to Green Park again," said Sattu.

"No way! I am too scared of speed, and the way she drives, even the seat belt struggles to put me back on the seat."

"You are going with her. Period," Sattu ordered, asking me to shut my mouth.

Sabotaging my life, I acceded to Sattu's offer. I lied to her again and we stuck to Sattu's military plan. It worked without any obstacle this time. I got a ride from her and history repeated itself. The roller coaster ride nauseated me. I couldn't talk much, but managed to get her phone number.

Next day she texted me if I wanted a ride. I couldn't say no and took the ride again. The same routine continued for over a week. I got used to those roller coaster rides. At the same time, I was feeling bad to lie to her every day. I practically did nothing at Green Park. She dropped me in front of a dental clinic which I lied I worked for part-time. I picked that particular clinic because it was right in front of the metro station. It was convenient to take the metro back home. Every day I entered the dental clinic and once she left, I took a swift exit. The clinic was busy, so I blended well with the patients without getting noticed by the receptionist.

Outside the clinic, there was a tea stall under a huge tree. After coming out of the clinic, I had tea at that very tea stall run by a fourteen-year-old-boy, Gopu. He was a lean, thin, dusky boy who was forced to give up his studies and run the tea stall after his father met with an accident. Gopu noticed me going in and coming out of the clinic every day. He asked me why I did that and I told him the truth. Gopu and I became good friends. After chatting with him, I took the metro back to my residence. It became a tiring affair after some time.

"I am done. This conversation is not going anywhere," I complained to Sattu, anticipating better advice.

"College Foundation day is next week. The college is hosting a DJ night. Get drunk and spill your emotions," Sattu suggested.

He provoked me again and I agreed yet again.

I texted Tanishq, asking if she would be attending the college function. She replied in the affirmative.

"Perfect," Sattu said as he got the news. "I will tell you how to approach her."

"I don't need advice this time," I replied, denying any kind of support.

For the first time, I decided to go impromptu. No planning, no advice, no preparation and no alcohol. Isn't that how love happens?

At the function, I saw her in a black saree, looking more gorgeous than ever. Everyone who was sober and not busy dancing, beheld her. She waved at me and joined Sattu and me at our table. I complimented her on her elegant look. She complimented me on my taste in fashion. After a few minutes of commending conversation, I kicked Sattu on his foot indicating him to leave. He left giving me a cold look.

I had a conversation with her over dinner. Then she expressed her love for alcohol and persuaded me to arrange for some.

I messaged Sattu and like a genie from the magic lamp, he arranged it within no time. We went to his car and they both got drunk with a significant amount of alcohol. Considering the ethical limitations of my job, I decided to stay sober. As a very characteristic trait of getting drunk, they both expressed the urge to hit the dance floor. I paid for being sober and was dragged too. I would have loved to dance with her, but she was not the only one on the dance floor.

"Why do you worry about others?" she asked, seeing my ineptness.

"I don't feel comfortable," I replied.

"Dance as if no one is watching you!" she screamed and pulled me to the dance floor.

I stood still to watch her for few seconds. I saw her swaying on the dance floor. She was true to her words, dancing like no one was watching her. I couldn't resist myself and tapped my feet to the tune. Within a few minutes, I was dancing like crazy, without worrying about the surroundings.

Tanishq left the dance floor a little later. Seeing that, Sattu interrupted my dance and whispered, "Tanishq went inside the college building. No one will be there. This is the perfect time to hit the bull's eye."

I managed to trespass the college garden to pluck a red rose to support my proposal. Sattu confirmed Tanishq was on the first floor. I saw her standing on the balcony, facing the other side. I reached closer to her. Due to the loud music, she couldn't hear my footsteps. I put the rose in the left inner pocket of my blazer before calling out her name.

"Tanishq," I said.

I had to raise the decibel to make my presence felt.

"Tanishq," I screamed.

She turned around and hugged me tightly. She had tears in her eyes and with her head on my chest she sobbed.

"What happened?" I asked worriedly.

She sobbed holding me tightly. She mumbled, "I am missing…"

The loud music and her sobbing didn't allow me to hear more than that. "Missing what…?" I asked.

"I am missing Varun," she said in a snuffled tone.

I didn't know who Varun was, but hearing that name from Tanishq hurt me. She entrenched her head into my chest for more comfort. I felt the rose being crushed inside my pocket. I recollected the grit and asked her again.

"Who is Varun?"

Busy crying, she didn't answer. I patted her head and stood silently, holding her, staring at the sky.

"This whole thing reminds me of my past," Tanishq mumbled, raising her head. Her teary eyes looked so beautiful. I could smell alcohol in her breath as she spoke, but she pretended to be sober.

"You want to go somewhere else."

"Hmm." She nodded.

I planned to take a walk with her outside the college campus, but as we walked to the parking lot, she suggested going for a drive.

"Can you drive?" she asked handing me the keys to her car.

"Sure I can. Where do you want to go?" I said grabbing the keys.

"Anywhere. Just take me away from here."

I opened the passenger door for her. Clueless, I drove the car. She was on the passenger seat, looking out of the window, wiping her tears. There was silence inside the car. Not that I didn't know what to say, but I was hurt knowing there was someone in her life that she still missed.

Tapping on the steering wheel and regaining courage I broke the silence, "Who is this Varun, your boyfriend?"

"My ex," she said, sucking in the tears. "We broke up a year ago."

It made me smile and I again looked towards the sky to pay my gratitude to the almighty.

"Sorry to hear that," I said, not being sorry at all. "How long ago did you break up?"

"It has been a while now, but I don't know why I cannot forget him."

"Recovery takes its own time. You will slowly forget him." I said asking the question that I wanted to desperately know the answer to. "Why did you dump him?" Adding a disclaimer. "Answer only if you are comfortable."

"He is an asshole. That motherfucker hurt me all the time. He is a confused piece of shit." This was the first time I heard a girl swear so much. Her ex-boyfriend was a jerk rant didn't finish there. She went on and on cursing the bastard. I focussed on the road and was all ears to her uncensored rant.

I drove to India Gate. The weather was beautiful and it was a crescent moon night. I wanted to make the most of it.

"Do you mind if we walk?" I asked her, slowing down the car.

She agreed to my offer. We parked the car and strolled towards India Gate.

We sat on the rock placed beside the pond. I positioned myself in a way that I could see the beautiful moon while talking to her.

"Do you have a girlfriend?" she asked.

"I used to have one when I was a student, but we broke up."

"Why did you guys break up?"

"She fell for some other guy."

"What a…" She stopped before saying the cuss word. Probably my reaction made her stop. She apologized immediately. "I am sorry, but I have a special hatred for girls who do that."

"It wasn't her fault. I could not manage to give her time and attention."

"So sweet of you to say that. But that is not true. If she loved you, she would have never given up on you, no matter if you gave her time or not."

"That is not hundred percent true. I never said that she cheated on me."

"She fell for a different guy while in a relationship with you. That is called cheating."

Our argument went on and on. She took an aggressive mode and persuaded me to believe that Noor had cheated on me.

We discussed jerks, bad relationships, and even dentistry. The only topic that was yet to be touched was love. I was looking forward to an excuse to begin talking about love but couldn't find any.

"You are an idiot," said my heart, "wasting time for no reason. Just say it."

"She is still not over her ex-boyfriend. Don't say it or else you will ruin your friendship," the more intellectual part of my body suggested.

This is what happens when you are in a dilemma. It appears like every object and every molecule of your body is giving you advice. That doesn't help; that only adds to the dilemma.

I got rid of the figments of my imagination that had been clouding my thinking capabilities.

"Let's eat some ice cream before everything closes," she proposed.

"Do you want to go to Baskin Robins?" I asked her.

"Who likes Baskin Robins? I like the mango candy. We can get it from the roadside vendor right here."

I was surprised by her choices. Looking at her and the way she was dressed, it was rather obvious that she came from a well-to-do family. But her choices were so elementary.

We went to the roadside vendor and got the last mango candy from his stock. It was around ten p.m. and everyone was shutting down. Seeing them all leave, I asked her where she wanted to go next.

"I want to stay," she replied.

Her response made me smile, but I had to hide it. I wanted to stay too, but didn't know how to ask her to stay.

"No one will be here after a while," I said.

"Isn't that more peaceful?" she asked.

We went back to the same rock. We sat there for another hour. We shared almost everything about ourselves – our dreams, our ambitions, our best friends, our favorites and our hobbies. She was fun to talk to. She not only laughed at my jokes, but also made me laugh. The night was perfect, but the only villain in my pseudo love story was time.

Her mom called her around midnight. I thought that was the end of my golden night. She freaked out by listening to the ringtone.

"We need to run to the car," she said as she rushed to the car.

Without asking any questions, I ran with her towards the car. She got into the car and started the car. For a moment I thought she would leave me behind and rush back to her place. Somehow I managed to follow her and sat in the passenger seat. The phone rang again. She turned on the music at full volume.

"Why are you…" I was about to ask her a question which she interrupted by pressing her palm against my blabbering mouth.

She then picked up the phone, her left hand still blocking my mouth. With loud music playing in the car, she had to yell to make herself audible.

"Hello mom," she yelled. "I am still at the college party."

My eyes widened, as she was using the loud music to support her lie. I was more shocked at the brilliance of her mind.

"I will stay at the hostel tonight and will come early in the morning," she continued.

Her mom brought the lie and was convinced. Tanishq was relieved. She hung up the phone and lowered the volume. Lastly, she released the lower one-third of my face from clutches of her palm.

"Yesss!" she yelled in excitement. "We can stay out the whole night."

"That is wonderful," I yelled too, raising my volume to match her excitement.

Having no clue about where to go and what to do, she drove the car. We made rounds of the inner and outer circles of Connaught Place.

Then our stomachs cried for some fuel and she proposed a drive to a famous 24x7 hour dhaba on NH 1 somewhere in Haryana.

"Don't you think that will be too far?" I showed my apprehension over her plan.

"It is only seventy kilometers from here."

"Seventy kilometers only to eat! Normal people don't do that."

"Normal is boring Dr Shiva," she said, accelerating the car. "Fasten your seat belt. This is going to be epic."

Before meeting her, I was just a normal guy who loved normal things. I liked following rules and she taught me how to break them. She lied at home, crossed the maximum permissible speed limit, danced like nobody was watching and drank without caring. She taught me how to live life. I sat on the passenger seat without holding the side rail and loved it.

She drove us to the dhaba and we had dinner. We sat outside, under the open sky. As the night passed by, the temperature began to fall down. I saw Tanishq struggling to keep her body warm. Like a real gentleman, I took off my blazer and wrapped it around her.

"Thanks, gentleman," she said.

She stared at my white shirt and saw the Superman impression on my chest.

"Do you always wear the superman vest?" she asked.

"Yes, I do."

"Why so?"

"Statistics say if you feel like a superhero, there are chances you behave like one."

She laughed at my virtual statistics. "I don't think that vest is helping you because you are so scared of speed."

"Not funny at all," I said sarcastically. "It also helps me save my abs from the world."

"You have abs?" she asked surprisingly.

"Yes, I do." I proudly said. I had lied, but only to impress her.

"That is impressive, Mr Abby."

She was impressed. But the whole night after that, I sat sucking my stomach in to support my lie.

"Us Punjabis, we don't have abs. We have flabs," she said, taking a big bite of an aloo paratha greased with butter.

"That is impressive too, Miss Flabby."

She laughed at our new nicknames – Abby and Flabby. She looked more adorable every time she giggled. I wanted to express my love to her. The crushed rose in my pocket had some hope that it might prove pragmatic tonight. The only barrier right now was her excitement. She was so elated about our night out that she didn't let me say anything. She talked continuously. I waited for a window which could provide me access to speak my heart. I failed again and again. She didn't take a pause. Finishing dinner, we drove back to Delhi. I volunteered to drive because she wanted to talk.

Tanishq fell asleep on the passenger seat. Maybe the Punjabi belly couldn't handle those parathas. She slept like a baby. I kept one eye on the road and another on the baby face she made while sleeping. The sun was on its horizon as the car entered Delhi. Without disturbing her sleep, I decided to drive to Green Park. I parked the car in front of the metro station and before waking her up, stared at her for some time. I wanted to capture that moment. I wanted to hold the night, but the speed with which the sun climbed the horizon was beyond my control. I could only stare at her. Her hands were packed inside my blazer which she still wore to keep her warm, her legs folded over each other on the seat and head tilted towards my side. I turned off the engine and the silence was priceless. The bicycle bells of newspaper boys and chirping of birds produced a beautiful melody. The first rays of sun fell on her face through the driver's side of the window and I was jealous of that sun ray. It touched her before me. Like a possessive lover, I blocked it by straightening my back and raising my head and shoulders to completely cover the window, but could not block it out. She also blinked her eyes and woke up.

"Good morning," she said stretching herself.

She saw the weird enlarged form of my body covering the window and she laughed again.

"Don't tell me you were on the Superman duty the whole night," she said.

She continued laughing. I regained the normal form as I rested my back on the seat.

"Oh god," she said as the sunrays blinded her.

"Now you know who was on Superman duty," I said.

"Abby please," she said blocking the sun rays with her cute little hands. "Please save me, Superman."

I went back to my Superman mode and covered the window.

"Where are we? What time is it?" she asked, bombarding me with questions.

"It is 5:40 a.m. and we are at Green Park. I will take the metro from here and you drive back home."

"Why at Green Park?"

"You don't live in Green Park?"

"No."

Her tongue came in between her teeth, indicating she had made a blooper. I figured out by her gestures that she had lied to me that she lived in Green Park.

"All this time you were lying to me? Where do you live?" I asked surprised.

"I live in Rohini."

"Rohini! That is entirely another end from here. That means you dropped me here and then travelled another hour to reach home?"

"Yes," she said looking away from me.

"But why did you do that?"

"To spend some time with you," she said, making a puppy face.

"What?" I said surprised.

Her eyes drooped down. Very slyly she admitted and I was still surprised. I pinched myself twice to confirm I was not dreaming. I wasn't. It was happening for real.

"I don't work in any clinic in Green Park," I said while looking down.

"What?" she reacted.

"I got to know from college records that you live in Green Park. So I made that up."

"I used to live here before. The college records still have my old address. But why did you do that?"

"To spend some time with you," I said, imitating her style.

"Oh god! You made me drive two extra hours for almost a week. Why didn't you tell me the truth?"

"Why didn't you change your address in the records?"

We both accused each other. Accusing each other was the best way to hide awkwardness.

"I think you should leave now. Your mom must be waiting for you. It will take you some time to drive to Rohini from here," I said.

"How will you go home?"

"I will take the metro from here."

I got down from the car expecting she would say something. She didn't. Very awkwardly we both said goodbye. She slid into the driver's seat and drove off. There was some time for the metro gates to open so I sat at Gopu's tea stall across the road and ordered some tea. I punched myself for being stupid.

"Idiot, you call yourself Superman. You are the biggest coward," my Superman vest talked to me. It seemed like everything around was laughing at my stupidity.

"Bhaiya? So early in the morning today? Why are you so worried?" Gopu asked me lighting an agarbatti at his tea stall.

"I did something stupid and now I regret it."

"Don't worry, everything will be fine. Believe in god. He will fix everything," he said pointing towards the poster of Lord Shiva hooked on the tree behind his tea stall.

I looked at the poster of Lord Shiva. Gopu asked me to bow my head in front of god. I did so and god was quick in responding. Tanishq came back again and parked her car right in front of me. I recalled that I had forgotten my blazer in her car. She got off the car and handed me the blazer. I looked into her eyes. Those beautiful eyes had a myriad of questions. They expected answers, but I stood still, declassifying my moronic image. I wore the blazer and thanked her for that.

"There is something in the pocket," she said.

I surveyed both the pockets. There was nothing. I shrugged my shoulders to indicate there was nothing.

"Check the inner pocket," she said folding her arms.

I slipped my right hand into the inner pocket and took the crushed rose out. The stem was crooked but firm and it had only one petal left. That one petal fought for the flower's pride and it was beautiful enough to sanction it as a symbol of love.

I grabbed the dying soldier with both my hands and went down on my knees.

"I am scared of the night and usually sleep through it instead of fighting my fear. But last night, for the first time, I wished to hold the night. I wanted that one night to stay forever. I don't know why. I hated the sun this morning to rise so early and ruining that dream for me. I hated it even more when it touched your face. I don't know why. And I don't know what am I saying right now, holding this crooked rose in my hands, but I am sure if you hold this rose, it will definitely smile too. That what Tanishq's charm is capable of doing – it can make a dead man smile."

She stared at me and tears oozed out of her eyes and rolled down her beautiful cheeks. She came towards me and held the rose. Then she went down on her knees and hugged me tightly. It seemed like the dead soldier had won the battle for me. She kept the rose with her.

Gopu witnessed the early morning romantic saga. He clapped and turned towards Lord Shiva's poster. He then looked at me and pointed his fingers towards the poster. Tanishq kissed me on my forehead and it seemed like my body had got recharged. I hadn't sleep the whole night, but still felt so fresh. I introduced her to Gopu. Her charm worked on Gopu too. He gave her a free cookie. Tanishq left with a smile. I was smiling like an idiot now.

"If I knew she is so beautiful, I would have asked her for myself. I prayed to god for you," Gopu said, jokingly.

"Don't worry. I will pray to god to send someone more beautiful into your life," I said.

"You better do," he replied with a smile.

All-my-tea God!

"Congratulations!" Sattu shouted as he got the news.

"It still feels like a dream," I said.

"Dating the hottest girl of college is always like a dream."

"I cannot wait to meet her."

"Are you going to take it slow or are you going back into the beast mode?"

"Shut up! She is not just another task for me. I love this girl and I am never going to get into the beast mode."

"I wish you learned from your past mistakes."

"I told you I was immature back then. This is pure love and I am mature enough to handle it."

"Doesn't matter how old you are. Falling in love with someone is like grabbing a knife and chopping a part of your heart and allowing it to leave your body. That is what love is," Sattu said seriously.

He was skeptical about love. He had never loved anyone in his life. Nor had he supported or encouraged any one of us to fall in love. Despite the fact that he helped me win Tanishq's heart, he was continuously warning me about falling in love.

"It is too late now. I am in love and seems like she loves me too," I announced.

"Good luck. But don't show your emotions. It makes you weak."

"What theory is that?"

"It is an extension of my fool-proof theory – nice men finish last. Once you show your emotions, you lose a girl. Emotions are a man's weakness. Keep that in mind. Love is a tunnel with perpetual darkness." His words were weird.

Sattu had all the time in this world to extrapolate new theories. Ignoring all his theories and statistics, I focused on my new beginning.

We were officially in a relationship now. We met only at the college. We couldn't find a chance to meet outside the college. She was kept busy by her parents on weekends. All the knowing each other conversation happened on the phone.

The college eventually became lovable and we started to look for places where we could meet without being spotted. Very soon the rumors of her and I having an affair fumed into the campus air. I was questioned by my colleagues if they were true. I decided to keep it a secret as the college rule book had deemed dating within the premises as illegal. There were rules to follow, but I was influenced by Tanishq's ideology – break rules and live free.

Every morning she came to my department making some excuse. She stayed there for one or two minutes. We both looked at each other from a distance and our eyes talked. As hard as I tried to conceal our relationship, the smile on my face did just the opposite. I smiled at a little glance from her and that was enough to reveal the secrets. Later in the day, I made excuses to enter the department she was posted in. I stayed there for the same duration and made eye contact with her. This game of hide and seek became our daily routine.

On a busy Monday, I waited for her routine entrance to our department. She missed her regular visit to my department. I went to her department and could not find her. I gave her a call.

"Hello," she answered. Her voice made it evident that she had just woken up.

"You are not coming to college?" I said.

"I slept too late last night. Don't feel like waking up."

"Why didn't you tell me before? I would have skipped it too."

"It isn't too late to bunk college," she said letting out a wicked laugh.

"I can take half day. Where do you want to meet?"

"I don't know. I will be home alone until evening today."

"That's good. I will make an excuse and take a half-day today and let's meet at the café in CP. Is that okay with you?"

"Yes yes, perfectly okay. But I am home by myself today. Both my parents are at work."

"That is good. Where do they work?" I asked, having no clue how that information was going to help me.

She didn't reply to my question and kept quiet.

"Hello, you there?" I asked again, "where do they work?"

"My head, Abby!" She said clenching her teeth, "Why are you so dumb?" She hung up the phone.

She had called me dumb! Then hundreds of questions popped up in my mind. She yelled at me and hung up. Come on, I was her teacher. My teacher ego got hurt. Wait, but hadn't I myself erased this boundary? I am just a professional senior. Still she should have respected that. Maybe I have passed that phase. I was her boyfriend now and she had all the rights to yell at me. Hang on! The most important thought popped at the end. Why was she mad at me? What did I do wrong?

I called her again seeking the answer.

Before I could say anything she started to cry. "I am sorry," she said.

"Hey, what happened?"

"I shouldn't have yelled. But I am missing you."

"I miss you too."

"Why don't you get the idea? I said there is no one at home."

"Yeah I got that part, but what is that supposed to mean?"

"Come to my place, dumbo!" she yelled again.

"Your place! But there is no one there."

"God! I am here, who else do you want?"

"Oh, I got it," I said, tapping my head. "Why am I so dumb?"

"Thank god. So are you coming?"

"Yes, I mean no. I still won't come."

"Why?" she asked.

"Your dad is a lawyer in the Delhi High Court. You have a loaded Beretta at home. There is no way I can jeopardize my life. Coming to your place means putting my nose in that barrel."

"The gun won't crawl towards you by itself. The one who pulls the trigger is not home," she said almost wickedly.

"What if he figures out that I was there?"

"How will he?"

"I don't know."

"Coward!"

She hung up on me again. I was left confused. As much as I wanted to be at her place, I was scared of her ruthless dad. She had told me how influential he was.

I accumulated some courage and looked for the excuse that could get me a half day off. Sattu expertly crafted a fake story to make the explanation look authentic. Not only that, he gave me his car keys so that I didn't waste time commuting by public transport.

"I am not giving you my car for no reason. I want you to come back triumphant in this car. You are going to conquer what had been unachieved so far," Sattu said juggling the car keys.

"Nothing like that is going to happen, but thanks anyway. I am only going to drive to meet her," I said, struggling to snatch the keys from him.

"Don't ruin the track record of my car. Every time this car has been driven to a girl's house, it has witnessed pride. This is not just a car, my friend; this is a victory chariot assembled with all the luxuries."

"Sorry to disappoint you, but nothing like that is happening today. Can I please have the keys now?"

"You have to promise me you will come back victorious."

"I want to come back alive. I am already nervous. Don't annoy me."

"Promise or public transport?" Sattu moved the keys away from me.

"Promise," I said, sighing away my frustration.

"That's my boy," he said, patting my back.

He handed over the keys. Tanishq texted me her address and I drove to her place. I was instructed to park the car at the nearby shopping complex and not in her apartment building.

I picked up her favorite chocolate and rushed towards her apartment building. Another set of instructions included the use of a fake name and phone number in the security register and not to use the elevators as they had cameras. It was no less than a mission. Why shouldn't it be? After all, I was about to trespass Advocate Batra's den without his consent.

The den was located on the third floor. I took the staircase and after climbing around three dozen stairs, finally reached the destination. I had to follow the third set of instructions here. Don't make any noise or else I will be spotted by her neighbour Sheila aunty, who was the human broadcaster of the apartment building. I walked on my toes to prevent any sound. I inched towards her apartment. The wooden door had a big metallic name plate saying 'Batras'. I knocked on the door and within a few seconds, she opened the door and pulled me inside grabbing my shirt.

"Yoohoo!" she shouted while I was fixing my shirt that she had crumpled while pulling me inside.

"You made it," she jumped in the air again. "It was easy, wasn't it?"

If only she would have noticed my sweaty shirt and pounding heart.

"Very easy," I said while my heart was still beating at twice the normal speed. I snuck into a dangerous premise of the city that was guarded by a Beretta.

She gave me a hug out of excitement and that hug made me forget the terror for a few seconds. With my eyes closed, I wanted to stay on her shoulders forever. But sometimes forever means few seconds. I opened my eyes and looked around her living room. A portrait of the owner of the house hanging on the wall caught my eye. Mr Batra's big eyes gleamed like they were warning me. 'Dare you touch my daughter!' The terror got reinstated and the heart pumped blood at a hastened pace.

"Can I get a glass of water?" I asked Tanishq.

"Sure, have a seat. I will get it."

Tanishq got a glass of water and I gulped it in one long draught. "More please," I said.

I emptied the second glass too in no time. My palms now pressed my thigh to stop my legs from trembling.

"Chill Abby," Tanishq said as she sat beside me on the couch. "You are safe."

My brain sent a message to the shivering control center that I was safe, but it was controlled by some other machinery. Deep down I knew I wasn't safe.

"I have snuck into the most treacherous place of the city. After an hour, I have to sneak out from here. If, by any chance, your dad gets any idea of this sneaking activity, my appointment with the bullet is sealed. How can you expect me to calm down?"

"Huh! Always overreacting for no reasons. Come here," she said pulling me towards herself. She hugged me and gently caressed me on my shoulders. The moment my shoulder felt her fingers, my body withdrew itself from the panic attack.

"Are you feeling good now?" she asked.

Why did she even ask that question? That soft touch had the power to revive life in a corpse. It took all the fear of bullets and the Beretta from my mind.

"You didn't come to college so that we could have this quality time?" I asked her.

"Abby, stop giving yourself so much importance," she said, pulling my cheeks, "I didn't go to college because my parent's bedroom's AC is not working and the repair guy was due to come this morning. All other family members were busy at work, so I took a day off. Sadly he hasn't come as yet. But I am glad you are here."

"Thanks to the impaired AC, I got a chance to be with you."

"That's true. You are like the reimbursement for that faulty AC," she said cutely, pulling my cheek. Then suddenly, she jumped up to her feet. "Since it is your first visit, I would like to show you my house."

"Sure," I said.

I followed her through the house tour.

"This is my dad's study room."

Each wall of the room had shelves and each shelf had books stacked vertically. On the majority of books, I could see Indian Penal Code inscribed. The center of the room had a very well organized giant study table with a miniature Indian flag. On one corner, there was a big iron coffer.

I knocked on the coffer with my knuckles and creating a melody of metal in the background I asked her, "what is this?"

"This is the most secretive stuff in my house."

"What is in it? Lots of money... some treasure..."

"I don't know. I am not allowed to touch it, but I am sure my dad keeps his gun in this coffer."

I snapped my hands from the coffer like I had got electrocuted. But the curiosity to see the gun couldn't stop me to ask her about the keys to that coffer.

"Get the keys. I want to see the Beretta. Can I see it please?" I asked.

"Dad carries the keys with him all the time. It is very private stuff."

"I wish I could see the gun."

"And I wish you never see this Beretta," Tanishq said.

The last and main attraction of her house tour was her bedroom.

"This is my room," she said with a passionate voice as if she was showing me the White House. The attraction of this bookless room was blue walls, blue curtains, blue bedsheets and blue cushions.

"This is beautiful. Is your favorite color blue?" I asked seeing the blue hue of her room.

"Yes. How do you know?" she asked curiously.

How did I know? There was so much blue in that room that if you leave a whale in that room, it would take a while to realize that it was not in the sea anymore.

"I just took a random guess," I said.

"It is royal blue, to be precise."

She then elucidated to me how royal blue is different from my version of blue. I barely listened to that. I was happy with my color dictionary that contained a measurable amount of colors.

Pointing towards her bed, I said in self-appreciation, "That must be the spot where you dream of me? Can I sit there?"

"It is all yours, feel free to sit."

I jumped on the cozy bed. She sat beside me.

"How can the host help you?" she said seductively while holding my shirt collar and pulling me towards her.

"Can I get some tea?" I said, pulling myself away from her.

"Sure. You can," she said, and pulled me closer, "anything else?"

"Also, if you can turn on the television please?"

"Anything else?" she said, biting her lower lip seductively.

"Pass me the TV remote too."

"Huh!" Tanishq scoffed and pushed me away from her. She threw the TV remote towards me and left for the kitchen.

Not that I didn't want to do anything mischievous, but I owed her an explanation about my past before even I kissed her. I was scared to lose her and that was the reason why I had not brought up my past till now.

I chased her to the kitchen and while she was struggling to find the ingredients, I was struggling to gather the courage to tell her about my past.

"What do you want now?" she said, opening the closets in the kitchen.

"I want to tell you something about my past. Before meeting you…"

"Before meeting me, I had no control over you," she said interrupting me, "so there is no point in knowing what you did or whom you dated. I know that after seeing me you haven't seen any other girl and in near future if you look at any other girl, then you better bear the consequences." She grabbed the knife and showed it to me as a warning. I smiled at her reply and a big burden gravitated from my shoulders. I wanted to kiss her but that knife was still in her hands. I calmed down my desperation.

"Go to the room now and let me make tea in peace," she instructed.

"Do you need any help?" I asked as I saw her helplessness with finding the ingredients. She refused any kind of help and sent me back to her room. I went back to television surfing.

After a long wait, she entered the room with an enormous blue mug.

I raised my right hand to bring the cup orifice towards my lips. She stared at me with enthusiasm. She had worked too hard to make tea and was curious to know what it tasted like.

Then came the moment when the tea touched my taste buds. The smart taste sensors didn't waste much time in judgment and made it clear – the tea was horrible.

The taste buds were about to give up after one sip. They described the tea as fabric color dissolved in hot water. But I didn't want to disappoint her.

"Wow!" I said with a smile, "it is amazing."

Tanishq smiled with pride.

"The best tea I've ever had," I added in appreciation.

"Thank you."

The smile she had on her face was priceless. I could have lied millions of times to see that million dollar smile. But deep inside my throat, the body was battling with each molecule of that tea. I looked at the size of the mug. At that moment, it appeared to be gigantic. Her smile gave me the courage to successfully pour the hot poison down my throat.

"Amazing!" I said as I sipped the last drop of tea.

"Do you want more?" she asked.

"I think I am good," I said politely.

"Now that you liked the tea, I want to tell you a secret. This was the first time I made tea. Isn't that unbelievable?"

Unbelievable! Someone who doesn't drink tea could have guessed that in a second. But that was not what I said to her.

"No way! You got to be kidding me? It seemed like you are a pro in making tea."

"I am a pro in making soup because that is the only thing I can make. Just for the record, I make the best soup in the world."

"Do you mind sharing your recipe with me?" I asked.

"It is a very secret recipe. My dad says this recipe is worth going on air. I can host my own soup cookery show."

"Can I get a preview of the pilot episode?" I requested.

"Welcome to *Cook It Up* with Tanishq Batra," she said joining her hands to imitate the cooks of those cookery shows watched by Indian mothers to please the taste buds of the guests. "First take two tomatoes and chop them into small pieces."

She cutely imitated the popular host from the show and explained the procedure to make her exclusive soup. The show lasted for fifteen minutes and before she could wrap it up, she added a surprise for her exclusive viewer.

"In today's episode, we will also demonstrate how to make the Tanishq Batra exclusive tea."

The viewer gave all his attention as he wanted to know all the ingredients that had gone into his belly.

"It is very similar to making soup, but instead of tomatoes and mushrooms, add water and milk. Sprinkle miracle powder for quality. Rest of the procedure is the same."

That miracle powder explained the miraculous sour taste to the tea. I stood shocked and applauded for her successful presentation. She took a bow in pride.

"What exactly is this miracle powder?" The viewer asked.

"It is a brown colored Ayurvedic powder my mom adds to everything she cooks. It doesn't give any taste, but it is very good for your stomach."

I gave her a thumbs-up in response to her miraculous confession.

The two of us wanted to utilize our time well. I locked my eyes with hers and ran my right hand over her cheek. She closed her eyes and I moved my lips closer to hers. She sat unmoved while I held her by her cheeks and planted a kiss on her forehead. She came closer to my ears and whispered, "I love you." Driven by emotions, we locked our lips and kissed for the first time.

Before we could take our love to the next level, the ethical section of my brain took over.

"It would not be fair," I said.

"What?" she asked.

"I mean… it is your parent's house and I've entered it without their consent. Now doing something mischievous to their daughter would be betraying their faith in you."

"Don't make me feel bad. I am not the kind of girl who would do anything like that."

"I know you are not. This moment is what should be blamed. This silence, your eyes, your fragrance and that kiss. Everything is driving me crazy. It's magic."

"You are too cute," she said pinching my cheeks.

"You don't trust me? Feel my heartbeat."

I asked her to place her head over my chest to listen to my heartbeat.

With her head on my chest, we lay on the bed with our eyes closed. I swirled my fingers into her soft hair and she played with the buttons of my shirt. We were awake, but dreaming. I cherished every moment of that dream until the dream was broken by a cracking sound of the doorbell.

DING-DONG!!!

"Who is that?" I said, scared.

"Don't worry. It must be the AC repairing guy. Don't come out of the room. I will show him the AC and he will leave in ten minutes or so," she said as she fixed her hair.

I followed her instructions while she left the room to open the door.

"Dad!" she yelled, loud enough to alarm me. "What a pleasant surprise!"

"I thought you went to college. I came here to attend to the AC mechanic," her dad answered in a robust voice.

"No, I stayed at home. I can take care of that."

As Tanishq answered him, she blocked the door denying his entrance to his own house. She did that to buy me some time to recover from the massive shock.

"Okay. I guess I can use this time to relax for a bit. I have to go back to work in an hour."

"But it is hot and your AC is not working. There is no point of relaxing here," she said.

Tanishq made another move to make him leave, but if the daughter was smart, the dad was smarter.

"That is right. But the AC in your room is working, so I will rest in your room."

I heard their conversation, thanks to his loud voice. I looked for an escape route and found nothing. I squeezed under her bed and watched Mr Batra walking inside the room. Tanishq followed him. I could listen to their conversation more clearly now. The long frilled bedsheet acted like a curtain to hide me. I was sweating profusely under that bed. It was claustrophobic. I messaged Tanishq that I was safe for now. She was relieved for a bit.

Her dad asked her to make the exclusive soup while he relaxed on her bed.

Tanishq brought some soup for him. I could hear every slurp.

"My daughter makes the best soup in the world," he said as he took the last sip.

"Thanks Dad."

"If it goes on air, you will make a lot of money," he said.

The fear of bullets and the Beretta forced me to join my hands, chanting god's name. The fear rose with every passing minute.

After spending some time under threat, I heard a loud sonorous sound – a sound enough to scare the hell out of me.

Boom!

Was it a bullet explosion from the Beretta? Did her dad fire a gunshot in the air to scare me? Thousands of such questions popped into my mind. I closed my eyes in anticipation of fear. The heart pounded with fear. I heard the sound again. It was as loud as a gunshot. It took me some time to realize it wasn't a gunshot. It was a fart explosion from Mr Batra. It wasn't a bullet; it was a gaseous bomb from a more powerful canon. He wanted Tanishq's recipe to go on air. Well, it didn't go on air, but evidently it went spreading in the air. His upset digestive system revealed the secret recipe of the soup to the atmosphere. The miracle powder miraculously diffused into the atmosphere. He groaned before firing the gaseous bomb and it seemed like the groaning sound was the trigger he pulled to fire a shot. Terrified, I managed to laugh at the situation. To control my laughter, I packed one end of my shirt into my mouth. The bombardment continued.

After continuous bombardment, my nostrcils smelt something terrible. It was the odour that usually follows such explosions. And it was brutal. I clutched my nostrils with my fingers. My tongue and food pipe were already paralysed by the toxic tea. It was my nostrils' turn to go inert. I suffocated under the bed. The shirt that was used to pack my mouth was used to cover my nostrils. These are the circumstances where death is on both the ends, and you don't know which way to go. The barrel of the Beretta was on the one end and the powerful canon on another. I had no clue where to go. I stayed under the bed holding my breath.

One hour and twenty-something farts later, her father got up from the bed and for work. I came out from under the bed and opened the window. I exhaled the contaminated air from my system and took a deep breath to rejuvenate my body tissues. Tanishq avoided eye contact to escape the embarrassment. She apologized for all the trouble but I didn't accept her apology. I was mad at her for the whole episode. I didn't want to visit her in the first place.

She had dragged me into it, and I had narrowly escaped death. I left her house without wishing her goodbye. As I walked towards the car, I realized that man has overrated a Beretta as a source to prove dominance; a misbehaving stomach is capable enough to destroy the opponent.

Karma's Punch

It was for the first time in our relationship that we didn't talk to each other for a week. She came to my department to make eye contact, but I ignored her. She called me numerous times, but I did not take her calls.

"Why do you blame her for that incident?" Sattu asked me.

"She was the one who called me to her place knowing the risks," I said.

"She called you because she was missing you. Her dad accidentally showed up. You are angry for no reason."

I knew I didn't have a valid rationale to get mad. What did I want to prove? Even if I did, this wasn't the right way of proving it. She wanted to talk to me as much as I wanted.

"Why don't you invite her over to our place? It is safe and convenient," Sattu suggested.

"This apartment had been an arena of lust. I want to maintain the sanctity of my love. Bringing her here means adding just another name to the list of visitors."

"Why are you so rigid about your concepts? She is over your past, so why can't you suck it up? Doesn't matter what we had done in this apartment, it has been a pure and pious place for me. I spent the best time with you and my other friends here. Don't you dare say a word against this apartment!"

I had never seen Sattu getting emotional before. I never thought he could be so sensitive about the apartment and his friendship with me. I felt an urge to hug him. He made me change my rigid concepts. I hugged him, for the first time sober.

Sucking up all the anger, I messaged her. It was too late now. She stopped attempting to ask for an apology. She didn't message me back. I invited her to my place. I left her my address and a note that I would miss college and wait for her at my apartment. She didn't reply, but I knew she would come. I cleaned my room and reopened the honeymoon suite, first time with a clean intention.

The next morning, she came. I apologized to her but she didn't accept it. She had a grumpy look on her face. I welcomed her in the same fashion like she had. I took her on a mini apartment tour. She followed me without talking. Then we sat in the honeymoon suite. I went close to her to recreate the magical moment. She got up from her chair and stood against the wall. I stood in front of her and tried to flick away the hair that fell on her eyes. She pushed my hands away from her. I held her shoulders and moved closer to her. She used all her force to shake me away, but I firmly advanced closer. I kissed her on her lips and moved a step back. She stood still for a moment and a second later she came towards me to hug me tightly. After a long hug, we passionately kissed and I slipped my hands gently into her neck. We surrendered ourselves to the magical moment. We kissed passionately while our hands mischievously undressed each other.

After some time, I realized there was no cover on our bodies. I glanced at her body from hair to toe. I realized I was holding the masterpiece of god. A body crafted with excellence, every curve finished with precision and texture ranging from very smooth to worth kissing. I took some time to appreciate the most wonderful craftsman. My eyes dug into her marvellous body and she shrunk a bit, allowing her arms to curtain her body. Mesmerized by the moment, I braced her wrists and pulled them away to remove the barrier. Her eyes stooped down. I moved closer to her to cover her body with mine. With the two bodies meeting each other, the two souls became one. The euphoria of the moment was incomparable. Never before had I felt as loved as I did that day. I felt connected to her.

Soon this became a daily affair. We bunked college often to stay at home. Sometimes we came to my apartment right after college. Love was at its pinnacle. She became good friends with Sattu and we began to hang out together.

"Let's have a party some day?" Sattu proposed.

"Aren't we having a party every day?" I said.

"Not this party. A proper party with music, alcohol and chicken," Sattu said.

"Yes. Let's do it," Tanishq said, giving a high five to Sattu.

"I am up for it, but no chicken. Music and alcohol are fine," I said.

"Please, we will have leaves too. You can hog on that," Sattu said, mocking my vegetarianism.

"There is no party without chicken," Tanishq said.

"But how is it even possible? We cannot have a party during the day and Tanishq cannot stay for the night," I asked.

"What if I take a night out permission from my parents? I will tell them I am staying in the girls' hostel with my friends," Tanishq said.

"Can you do that?" I asked.

"Sure. The only hiccup is that if, by chance, my dad calls the warden, we will be in deep trouble," Tanishq said.

"Don't worry about the warden. I will take care of her," Sattu said.

"Can you? How?" Tanishq asked.

"Maybe your boyfriend didn't tell you about my legacy. When it comes to convincing a female, no matter what age she is, I do it with ease," Sattu said.

"Sir, can you please explain it to me?" Tanishq asked him again.

"Don't even ask. He will start telling you some boring made-up stories. If he says he will take care of it, that means he will. I trust him with that," I said.

How he did that, we don't know till date, but he convinced the fifty-year-old warden of the girls' hostel and made her believe that Tanishq was staying in the hostel for the weekend. We made a hoax call to the girls' hostel to ask whether Tanishq was in the hostel and the warden said yes. This was our way to check if Sattu's charm had worked. It worked and we didn't ask him how.

I used my hand-made paratha as bait for Tanishq to stay away from chicken that night. She agreed. Sattu, as usual, took care of the party arrangements. He stuffed the refrigerator with bottles of vodka, beer, and whiskey. He got a cake that had 'Welcome Tanishq' written on it. He wanted to celebrate her as our new unofficial roommate. He brought a big shiny 'Friends Forever' banner that he pasted on the wall of our living room.

After college, the three of us came to our apartment. We started to drink straight away. The party started with cutting the cake. I didn't let them cut the piece that had 'Tanishq' on it. I wanted to keep her name shining on the cake. Within no time, only that quarter piece of cake was left on the tray. Then we painted faces with the cake, which was followed by shots of tequila, loud music, and crazy dancing. It was a treat to see Tanishq dance again.

As always, Sattu left the apartment after being drunk. Whom does he call after getting drunk was still a mystery. It surprised Tanishq as well.

"Where did he go?" she asked me.

"I have no clue. He does that every time he gets drunk. He makes a call to someone. None of his friends know who that is," I replied.

"Is that his ex-girlfriend?"

"I have no clue. I have known him for five years and he has never talked about it. So let's keep it a mystery. He will be back in an hour or so."

"Abby, that means there is no one home," she said, winking at me.

I had heard about the aphrodisiac quality of alcohol, and that day, I observed that effect on her. We went inside the honeymoon suite and utilized this quality of alcohol as much as possible. After some time, her Punjabi appetite kicked in and she asked for parathas. Like an obedient boyfriend, I went to the kitchen to cook for her. I had a tipsy feeling, sufficient enough to make my head spin. Plus, I had a pressure to cook delicious parathas to win Tanishq's heart. I sobered myself up to concentrate on my cooking skills. Tanishq relaxed inside the honeymoon suite, texting me at frequent intervals.

Tanishq: *I am hungry.*

Me: *You just ate me. What else do you want?*

Tanishq: *Something vegetarian and delicious ;). Probably a paratha.*

Me: *Ouch! :(It is going to be the best paratha of your life. Good things take time.*

Tanishq: *Ok Mr Perfectionist. I am waiting.*

She sang from the room in her drunken voice to entertain me. I laughed as I was flipping the paratha.

Me: *Food is ready. Come outside, lazy bum.*

Tanishq: *I am not lazy. I am cold and nude.*

Me: *Wow. I think I should come inside. ;)*

Tanishq: *Shut up. Give me something to wear.*

Me: *Can you check in my closet, please? Wear anything that you like.*

I finished cooking parathas and brought them out on the dining table. I set the dining table and texted Sattu to come for dinner.

"Come out, Flabby," I shouted.

I didn't get any response from her. I knocked on the door and still didn't get any response. Curiously, I opened the door and entered the room. I saw Tanishq sitting with her head down, facing the other side. She wore my hoodie. I called out to her again, but she didn't reply.

"Is everything okay?" I asked.

Nothing. I went in front of her and clapped twice to grab her attention. She was still unmoved. She raised her head and I saw a diary on her lap which she was busy reading. It was the dirty journal that had all the competition details between Sattu and me. Tears flooded her face while she read the journal. I snatched away the diary from her hands.

"Give me a chance to explain please," I said, taking away the journal from her hand.

"So I am just a competition for you. Just another fucking number, right?" she said clenching her teeth.

"No, no, not at all. I love you, Tanishq."

"Shut up. Don't you fucking dare say that," she yelled at the top of her voice.

"It was just my past," I said.

"I told you I don't care about your past," she yelled.

"Then why are you yelling? This diary is meaningless."

She snatched the diary back from me and showed me the page on which her name was written and then scratched out.

"You won the bet. Why don't you enter your experience in this?" she said.

"Tanishq please…"

"Don't say a word," she grabbed a pen and began to write, "What could you say about me? I was just another dumb girl whom you brought to bed."

I snatched the pen from her hands.

"Give me one chance to explain," I yelled.

"Shut up," she shouted with double the intensity and threw the diary at me. It hit me on my face, right above my left eye. "I was such a fool to fall for you."

She grabbed her cell phone and car keys and left my apartment. I ran after her. She sat in her car and turned on the engine.

"Please don't drive, you are drunk," I said knocking on the window.

The car was locked from inside. On neutral, she accelerated the car to its full capacity to display her distress. The engine revved and without looking at me, she changed the gear and zoomed past.

Sattu came back and asked me about Tanishq. He saw me crying and threw many questions like what, why, where and how. I told him about the incident.

"I am so sorry. It is my fault. It was me who hid the diary in that closet. No one was using the suite at that time. I didn't know that anyone would ever find that journal," Sattu said, sloshed.

"Now that makes sense. You hid it in my closet. You are the one who invited her to this party. You are the one who wrote her name in the journal. It was a set up by you. You liked her too, right? You did it on purpose."

"Don't be silly. You are drunk," he said while shaking his sloshed head.

"I am not drunk. Look at me," I said slapping him softly to grab his attention. "Look at me. You still like her, right? You did it on purpose?"

"Don't be foolish. Why would I do that?" he said struggling to stand still.

"Because you are selfish. You can never be loyal to anyone, not even to your friends."

"Nandu, you are drunk and hurt right now. Stop making assumptions. Call her! I will clarify the misunderstanding."

"You bloody liar!"

He was right. I was hurt and drunk. I didn't know what I was saying. I was upset with myself, but I needed someone to blame. Sattu was my scapegoat, and I snapped at him. But verbal assault wasn't enough. I couldn't control the impulse and charged at Sattu with my fist. Sattu couldn't take the blow and fell on the floor. He got up, rubbed his eyes and propelled back at me. We grabbed each other by the collar and assailed each other against the wall. The big shiny 'friends forever' banner tore down in the process. So did our friendship.

The fight came to an end as my phone rang. Usually, in the middle of an intense fight, I would have cared less of a ringing phone, but I assumed it might be Tanishq and I dropped a final kick to throw Sattu away from me.

I looked at the screen on the phone. As expected, it was Tanishq calling. I swiped the phone screen to the right.

"I am so sorry Tanishq," I said. "Please give me a chance to explain."

I continued to apologize without listening to anything.

"Hello," a coarse manly voice answered.

"Who is this?" I asked.

Before I could get an answer, Sattu got up and yelled in a drunk tone.

"Tanishq, your boyfriend has gone mad…"

To shut him up, I pressed my hand against his mouth and sandwiched him against the wall.

"This is Advocate Batra, Tanishq's father," the man on the other side of the line replied.

I was shocked for a moment. I would have hung up, but it was too late.

"Hello sir. How are you?" I said in a shaky voice, my hand still squeezing Sattu's mouth.

I expected Advocate Batra to be rude and mean to me. His voice indicated something else. He was soft and generous to me.

"Tanishq met with an accident," he said.

"What?" I said shocked. "How is she? How did that happen?"

"She is fine. There are minor injuries. She is in the hospital."

"Which hospital?" I asked.

"I am sending my driver to pick you up."

"I can come on my own sir. Tell me the address please."

"I will send someone. I got your address from Tanishq. My driver will be there in around half an hour."

"Thank you sir," I said.

I hung up the phone. Meanwhile, Sattu bit my hand to release himself. I shook my hand to calm down the pain. I looked at Sattu. He was still in the mood to fight. I explained to him what had happened. He showed concern, but we didn't talk to each other. I had other things to worry about. I didn't know why her father wanted to meet me. Maybe he had figured out that Tanishq wasn't staying at the hostel. But why was he so polite? At that time, many questions surrounded me. But I was more concerned about Tanishq. I washed my face and I wore a white kurta-pyjama to look decently presentable in front of her dad.

I waited outside for his driver while Sattu got busy in cleaning the mess made by our fight. I saw two headlights approaching our apartment. Surprisingly, it was a police Jeep. Two constables came out of the jeep and asked me to get inside. Was I being arrested? What the hell was going on? I called Sattu to rescue me. He talked to the two constables. He was pretty charged and yelled at them. He was arguing with them for me. I felt ashamed of my behaviour. I was ready to kill this man and he was risking his life to save me.

The argument between them took a serious turn. Sattu tossed his knowledge about the Indian Penal Code. He didn't have much knowledge about the law, but when people yell in English, they are taken more seriously. The two constables lowered their volume and took him seriously. They explained to him that they were sent by Advocate Batra to pick me up. They would drop me to the hospital.

I sat in the police Jeep and Sattu insisted on joining me. I wanted him to come too, but alcohol in his system and his short temper could create problems in front of Tanishq's family. Moreover, I didn't want to give her family a shock by making it obvious that their daughter was staying over with two drunk guys. One drunk guy would be enough of a shock for one night. I asked him to stay at home.

The constable drove me to a very strange place, which could be anything but a hospital. I asked them many questions, but they didn't say a word. The huge building was the Delhi Police Headquarters. I was welcomed by Tanishq's dad at the front door.

"Dr Shiva?" he asked.

"Yes sir," I replied.

"I am Tanishq's dad, Advocate Batra."

I bent down to touch his feet. He didn't react. He walked inside the building and instructed me to follow him. I walked behind him, scared. I asked him many questions about Tanishq but he stayed mute. His expressions gave me an idea that it was not going to be a pleasant visit.

He walked into a chamber where I could see an officer of IPS rank. He asked me to take a seat. I sat in front of the officer while Advocate Batra sat beside me.

"What is the matter sir?" I asked.

"Was Tanishq with you?" the officer asked.

I didn't say anything. I wasn't sure whether they knew the truth or not. The officer repeated the question.

"Yes sir. She was with me." I said.

"How do you know her?" he asked.

"I am her teacher, sir," I said.

"Since when is this going on?" Advocate Batra asked.

"There is nothing like that. You got me all wrong," I said as I turned towards him.

"Shut up!" Advocate Batra yelled. "Answer only what is asked."

Now I know where Tanishq got that bad temper from. It runs in the family. I wanted to say I love your daughter, but that would be inviting more danger.

"We are good friends," I said.

I felt tormented by him and sought some help from the IPS officer who witnessed this torture. But it turned out that they both were good friends. Soon I realized that it was a set-up to trap me. He didn't want to meet me. He wanted to warn me. The dark and dingy police headquarters didn't scare me. Her father bashing me didn't scare me either. I was still concerned about Tanishq.

I didn't look at her father. I sat bending my head, avoiding any eye contact.

He wanted me to fear him, but I showed no signs of fear. I was worried. He played his last card to scare the crap out of me.

"Officer, what charges can we lay on him?" Advocate Batra said to his friend.

I looked up at him, shocked and scared.

The officer took a deep breath, adjusted his fat belly in the revolving chair and as he spoke, he played with the crystal paperweight on his table.

"Kidnapping, intoxicating a girl, attempt to rape, and some other charges. In total, we are looking here for a minimum of seven-year imprisonment. All you have to do is lodge an FIR."

What the hell! I looked at him shocked and scared. That was enough to make me cry. For the first time that night, I forgot Tanishq. All I could see was me standing behind bars, my parents crying for me and my career being flushed down the toilet.

I whimpered like a girl. I pleaded in front of the officer, expecting mercy.

"I haven't lodged an FIR yet," Advocate Batra said holding a piece of paper that read 'First Information Report' in bold letters. He slipped his hands into his pocket to bring out his pen.

"Sir please," I said wiping my tears and holding his hand to stop him from writing. "I am so sorry sir. I didn't do anything wrong."

"Let go of my hand," he said as he uncapped his pen.

I fell at his feet and begged for mercy. "I am sorry sir. Please don't fill the FIR. I will be ruined."

His face showed the feeling of triumph as I cried helplessly. He put the cap back on his pen. He grabbed my hair and pulled my head up.

"It is because of you that my daughter lied to me. It was because of you that she met with an accident. Her car hit a tree. Luckily she is safe, but what if something had happened to her? I would have ripped you apart," he said.

Tanishq was in an accident. That called for a drunken driving case, but thanks to our system, she was safe at home, and the one who hadn't ever killed even a mosquito was being averred. I was sure her smart dad played with the law to get her out of trouble. That wasn't my concern, though. At that moment, I didn't care who was punished or not. I didn't care about the loopholes of the judiciary system. I was solicitous about saving myself.

The officer turned towards me and said, "I don't want to see you around that girl or anyone else at least in my area. We have a Romeo cell in this station. You cannot even imagine what happens inside it."

He called his constable to escort me out.

"Gangaram, throw him outside," he ordered, "and bring two cups of tea soon."

The constable was the only person who looked more like a human in that corrupt building. The old man with gray hair and thin stature, Gangaram was soft spoken and seeing me cry he patted my back. He took me to the tea stall from where he was supposed to get tea for his boss.

"Come here, let us have tea," he said as he offered me a seat beside him on a bench.

I was crying. He ordered a cup of tea for me.

"Stop crying. I heard what happened inside. You look like an educated young guy. I can see you come from a nice family. These are all rich people. These people rule this country. They make their own rules and ask us to follow them. Don't meddle in their lives. Study and take care of your family," Gangaram said.

Gangaram's words didn't mean anything at that moment, but he had told me the bitter truth of our society. 'Ruled by rich people.'

I finished my tea and left the police headquarters. Sattu continuously called me to know what happened, but I switched off the phone. I didn't want to go home. I needed some time alone to overcome the terrible nightmare. I walked on the streets of Delhi aimlessly.

Tired and sleepless, I reached home in the morning around 6 o'clock. I saw a moving truck in front of our apartment. Sattu was outside, guiding people to move his stuff.

"Are you moving out? Are you still mad at me?" I asked him.

"Where were you all night?" he said.

"It is a long story. First tell me why are you moving out?"

"We both are moving out."

"What!"

"The landlord was here this morning. He gave us a notice to vacate within twenty-four hours. He didn't give any reasons, but he was furious."

"But why all of a sudden?"

"He said we bring girls over and this is a reputed society."

"I don't know why I think that Tanishq's dad got us kicked out."

"You think?" he asked, "Can't you see? He made it all happen. Our landlord was the coolest man we ever met. He always knew what we did behind those windows, but all of a sudden he had this epiphany that this was a reputed society!"

More than me, moving out would hurt Sattu as he was more emotionally attached to that house. He packed my stuff into the moving truck and sent it to his cousin's place for the time being. We both went inside the apartment for one last time. We walked inside all the rooms and quietly cherished old memories. It was the first time in my life I saw Sattu cry. He went to his room and hugged the wall and broke into tears. I couldn't be less ashamed of getting us kicked out. We hugged each other and locked the doors. The domain of our friendship was locked forever. A big nine-lever metallic lock swung on the front door. We handed the keys to the landlord. He felt sorry for kicking us out, but he was helpless.

"This apartment is jinxed. Vaastu can never be wrong," the landlord said as he took the possession of keys.

We both sat in our car and left for Sattu's cousin's place who had agreed to keep us at his home for two days. I drove the car while Sattu sat looking away from me. He was quiet and looked out of the window throughout the journey. I saw him wiping his tears a couple of times.

The next day when I went to college, I was called by the Dean. She wanted to see me in her cabin.

"You were one of the best faculties we had. I didn't expect this from you," she said.

There was more to the suffering. She told me how I brought shame to her institute.

"You broke the code of ethics. Dating a student is against the rules. I am sorry but you are being expelled from your services with immediate effect," she said, pressing her right hand hard to stamp my expulsion letter.

I left her office with a piece of paper that could decide my future. I didn't get a good character certificate. I didn't get a proper farewell from the staff either. The news soon voyaged through the campus. The students bunked their classes to bid me a final goodbye at the college gate. Some of the sensitive ones cried. Some tough ones wanted to revolt, but I stopped them. I didn't wish to stay there anymore because I wouldn't be able to face Tanishq anyway.

I left the college and later that night, grabbed my stuff from Sattu's cousin and left the city. I went back to my hometown Nainital.

I remembered Keshu had once said that my karma would follow me. This was the moment I realized he was right. I lost my girlfriend, my best friend, my apartment and even my job. Karma had punched me hard.

Miracles

I returned home devastated. My parents were surprised to see me back home. They always wanted me to work in my hometown and I had been avoiding their offer since the past one year. I didn't tell them why I was home. I said I took some time off from work. They were excited to have me back. But at the same time, they unendingly asked me about my future plans. Staying at home became tough as I was continuously bombarded with questions. I decided to give my volunteering services to the dental wing of the district hospital. The busy hospital kept my mornings engaged and helped me avoid answering my parents at home.

I had stopped texting Tanishq. I never bothered to ask her how she was and what she was doing. Neither did she show interest in my whereabouts. I missed her and wanted to talk, but was scared of the consequences.

The days were spent in the hospital with the patients, but the nights were terrible. The urge to speak to her peaked during the darkest hour. The terror of that one crazy night calmed all the urges and prevented me from contacting her.

When every door was closed in a blitz, another opportunity knocked my door. During my internship, while my parents were nagging me to do something productive with my life, to calm their desperation, I applied to a Canadian University for higher studies. The university confirmed my admission and granted me a scholarship too, that made the studies affordable.

My parents were excited and proud of me. I accepted the offer and applied for the study visa. The visa was also approved smoothly. I had a month's time to pack my stuff and leave for Canada. I was excited and elated about a new beginning, but needed to know about my equation with Tanishq. Undoubtedly, her father's threat scared me, but that didn't stop me from loving her. Not even a single day went by when I didn't think about her. I wanted to give the news to her, but didn't know how to. She was probably mad at me, for I was yet to give her any clarifications.

My flight tickets were booked. The flight was due to depart from New Delhi. I contacted my three best friends to meet me at the airport on the night of the departure.

Meanwhile, there were celebrations at my house. My mom started making some sweets for me to take abroad with me. She knew I would miss homemade food so she made sure to pack snacks that would last for about three months. All these sweets and snacks came with a motherly warning – 'it is exclusively for you, don't share them.' She was scared to send me to a foreign country where I knew no one. My mom tied three saffron-colored threads on my wrist for extra safety in a strange land. It made my wrist heavier by a few grams, but I didn't say no to this antivirus threading. When there were countable days remaining for me to leave, she took me to the temple every day. Every day she wrapped her dupatta over her head and joined her hands and closed her eyes in front of the idol. Then she chanted something and placed her hand on my head to transfer all the blessings she earned from her conversation with god. I stood there not to pray to god, but to wonder at my mom's innocence. Her faith in those blessings facilitated me to believe in miracles.

My father was busy writing letters for me to read when I reached Canada. He had this unique way of transferring his wisdom to me. He didn't talk much, but he wrote letters to me. The letters were usually inspiring and motivating and most of the times made me cry. He started writing to me when I moved out of my home. I kept all his letters and whenever I felt drained of inspiration, I read them.

Between all these preparations…where was I? I was hiding my misery behind a big fake smile. The excitement of admission blew away the air of melancholy for a brief period. I was soon going to pursue my dream of studying Forensic Odontology in Canada. I was excited to some extent, but a more important concern was Tanishq. I was desperate to contact her. Every day I rolled my fingers around the godly threads tied around my wrist in the hope of a miracle. Every day, it went in vain.

The day of my departure arrived. I reached the airport with two big suitcases. My parents accompanied me too − my father with some worries and mother with a round thali. The metallic thali contained a diya, a copper bell, some rice and lots of red powder that would soon be pasted on my forehead with one gentle vertical stroke.

Sattu, Shardul, and Keshu met me at the airport. All three of them congratulated me.

"Where is my farewell gift?" I asked.

All of them nodded.

"Cheapsters," I said, "you guys didn't bring a gift even today?"

"We don't believe in materialistic gifts," Shardul said.

"Don't try to cover up. I won't bring anything for you guys when I come back."

"The gift that we got for you has the capability to force you to stay in India," Keshu said.

"Nothing much is left here for me. I don't think anything can force me to stay now. Where is the gift anyway?"

"It was too big to carry in my pocket, so I sent it inside the airport. You will find it before boarding the plane," Sattu said.

"Are you joking?" I said, raising my brows.

"Yes, he is. Now don't waste time. Your parents are waiting for you," Keshu said.

I hugged all three of them and moved to seek blessings from my parents, who accompanied me till the first walk through the metal detector. One either required a visa or influence to enter beyond this point. I touched their feet and my mom circulated the thali in a clockwise direction a few times. She chanted a few mantras for my safe journey. With her other hand, she shook the bell. The sound was loud enough to attract attention of every passer-by. I closed my eyes and said my prayers to god. With watery eyes, they said goodbye. I controlled my tears in front of them, but as I entered the airport, I broke down and cried in one corner.

Since my vision was blurred by the tears, I couldn't see a figure approaching me. I rubbed my eyes to clear the vision and saw a familiar silhouette. It was Tanishq standing in a red salwar-kameez. I rubbed my eyes again, even slapped myself. To confirm it wasn't a dream, Tanishq slapped me on my left cheek.

"You are leaving the country and didn't even tell me," she complained.

"How come you are here?" I asked.

Before I could take a guess, I received a text message from Sattu.

Hope you got your farewell gift. All the best.

"Sattu sir told me everything about that diary. I am sorry I overreacted. He mentioned about your admission too and gave me the flight details. That is how I am here," she said.

I was moved by Sattu's efforts.

I hugged Tanishq. At that moment, I wanted to miss my flight and stay in India.

"Why didn't you inform me before?" she asked.

"Your dad warned me to stay away from you."

"I am sorry. That night I was drunk and crashed my over speeding car into a tree. The cops came and I had to call dad. He figured out that I wasn't in the hostel. And then I had to tell him the truth. He got overwhelmed and wanted to meet you."

"It was a terrible night for me as well. I don't want to talk about it."

"Yeah. Good thing he didn't meet you. He only warned you over the phone."

"Who told you that?"

"My dad told me. I didn't think your love was so weak. My dad gave you a normal concerned threat and you stopped calling me! That is your weakness. You don't fight back. Fight for what you love."

From her statement, I realized her dad hadn't narrated the complete story to her. I didn't want to portray her father as a villain and took the blame yet again.

"I am sorry. I get scared too easily," I said.

"It's ok. Be brave. I am with you," she said patting my back.

Only if she knew how terrifying that normal concerned threat had been.

"Why are you leaving?" she said holding me tightly.

"I can tear the ticket, if you say," I said pointing towards my plane ticket.

"No, don't do that. This is what you always wanted to do."

As we hugged each other, a very sweet voice announced the boarding for my flight.

"I have to leave now," I said.

She walked me to my luggage check-in. I kissed her forehead and said goodbye. She stood there as I walked through the metal detector. I was on the other side now. She waved me a final goodbye.

I walked towards the flight. Hold on, I forgot to ask her something. I returned back to the metal detector.

"How did you enter the waiting lounge?" I yelled. The CRPF official gave me a stern look and warned be to be softer. I whispered in his ear, "Girlfriend." He just smiled and let me talk.

Tanishq raised her imaginary collar in pride. It was her way of showing how influential her father was. Being Advocate Batra's daughter was enough to gain access to the waiting lounge. I smiled at her and walked towards the gate.

The miracle had happened. Tanishq was back in my life. My relationship had survived the first big drift, but the second hiccup was about to follow soon. A very long distance relationship would be the next challenge. The three beautiful air hostesses sought my attention as they spread their arms to demonstrate emergency combat. I totally ignored them as I focused on the ways to combat a very long distance relationship.

Hate Thy Neighbor

I reached a very infamous town of Canada called Sudbury. It was a small town with a very limited population owing to its notoriously cold weather. In the heart of the town was located the Laurentian University where I was going to begin my new journey.

I was received by the university officials at the airport. They brought me to the university residences where I was allotted an apartment. The hostels in Canada are called residence and they are totally different from the ones in India. There is no separate hostel for girls and boys and you don't share your room with anyone. In my residence apartment, there were two rooms – a shared living room and common kitchen. The residence was allotted according to the program opted for in the university and for convenience, they are to be shared with a classmate. In my case, I had to share it with another International student who was not from India.

I wasn't given any details of my residence-mate. I grabbed the keys and entered my apartment. It was a beautiful apartment. I was allotted room A. The room B resident was yet to arrive. I jumped onto my bed and to overcome my jet lag, I slept. I woke up after almost twenty hours. I had never thought that travelling to a different part of the world could be that exhausting.

It took me some time to regain my senses and figure out that I was in some other country. I was feeling dazed from the long sleep and fatigue of travelling across the globe. I walked out of my room rubbing my eyes. In search of food, I walked towards the kitchen. The main door to the apartment was open and there was a big maroon briefcase in the corridor. The maroon briefcase had a metallic lunchbox on top of it. The scenario wasn't acceptable at all, as it invited suspicion. I remember when I walked in to sleep, there was nothing in the living room. I went close to the briefcase. With a black marker in bold letters, a name was printed on the briefcase – 'Madiha Kashif Siddiqui'. The name sounded a bit unusual. The other side of the briefcase was occupied by an address. Out of a long address, I moved to the bottom most line that said Lahore, Pakistan. I got scared of the lunchbox and the briefcase. I had watched documentaries on television where they show how a lunchbox is used to trigger bomb blasts. The hysteria broke down when I heard the beeping sound. It was a continuous beep that confirmed that it was a time-bomb and could blow any moment. I ran outside my apartment, panicked and ran towards the main desk to inform the resident officials about the bomb. They immediately called university security and rang the emergency alarm. The residence building was evacuated right away. The security teams questioned me over and over whether that was a bomb or was it a nightmare. I confirmed it was a bomb. All the residents came out of the building and the cops and fireman entered the building. They asked me about the location of the bomb. In around half an hour the cops came out with the lunch box and an alarm clock. It turned out to be my roommate's briefcase and lunch box. It was termed as a hoax call and the residence apologized in writing. I was amused by my stupidity but the security team called it an act of awareness and patted my back. My tired brain had imagined an extreme situation.

I received commendations for my bravery. Where I became famous amongst the residence, one person became the anti-hero. It was my roommate – Madiha Kashif Siddiqui, all the way from Lahore. She was chided by the security team for leaving her briefcase in the corridor. In her defence, she said she had gone out to a phone booth to make an urgent call and the alarm clock was set as a reminder to make that call. The officials still bashed her. She felt very humiliated. Even though I knew it was my fault, but I did not have guts to turn myself in front of the angry officials. I preferred to celebrate my fake heroics.

Once the two-hour hoax show came to an end, I approached her to apologize. Her briefcase was brutally torn apart by the security personnel and all the stuff inside lay on the floor. When I entered the apartment, she was trying to collect all her stuff. It included her clothes and photographs of her family. She sat on the floor on her knees and as she grabbed the photograph of her parents, she cried. She tried to hold her tears when the security was bashing her, but she couldn't hold them back now. I stood behind her and witnessed her conversation with her parents' photographs.

"You were right Ammi, I shouldn't have come to this country. You were right… people are not nice here. They look at us with suspicion," she said holding her mother's photograph close to her heart.

I couldn't have felt worse. I didn't have the nerve to apologize either. I stood behind her feeling compunctious.

She broke down, sobbed and cursed herself for leaving her homeland. I poured some water into a glass and approached her.

"I am really sorry," I said, passing her the glass of water.

She sobbed as she turned towards me. She looked nowhere close to a Pakistani – natural golden hair, fair skin, hazel eyes that shone at that moment owing to the tears – she looked more like of Caucasian ethnicity. Lord, she was unexceptionally pretty. I was awestruck.

No matter how pretty she was, after all, she was a Pakistani. I had something against them. I didn't like them. Aren't they all bad? Yes, they are. That is what I was told when I was in India.

"I am really sorry," I said.

I wasn't really sorry because that is what they have been doing in India. That was one of the rarest lunch boxes as it had no explosive.

"I am really very sorry," I said for the third time.

She didn't take the glass of water from me. I kept the glass and tried to help her collect her clothes from the floor into her ripped briefcase. She refused any sort of help. She wiped all her tears, collected all the clothes and walked into her room. To show the resentment, she shut the door on my face. I concluded that she was angry beyond repair. I didn't care much. I took a sip of water from the glass and went into my room.

She went to the officials next day with a request to change her residence apartment, but was forced to stay for at least one semester. Since we had to share the kitchen and living room, she drew a line with white chalk to separate her portion from mine. I called that line the LOC.

She hated me for what I did, but I hated her for some unknown reason. Why did I hate a beautiful girl like her? Because I was a loyal boyfriend? Or because she was rude to me? Or because she was a Pakistani? Maybe the latter....

The line of control was drawn between us and hatred lay on both the sides. The refrigerator was definitely the Kashmir of our residence. It had apples, it had ice, it smelt amazing and it was the disputed area. There was no LOC in the refrigerator. We both fought over the refrigerator space.

The battle wasn't limited to the residence. It went on in the college as well. Since we both were in the same class, we had disputed sessions inside the lecture hall as well. We both were the only two students from the subcontinent. The three other international students were from China. The rest were Canadians.

She got on my nerves. She cooked non-vegetarian in the kitchen which created chaos in my Brahmin nostrils. She listened to music at an indecently loud volume. Her choice of music was old Pakistani folk songs. It sounded so dated I am sure Mr Jinnah would have played it on his gramophone to celebrate Pakistan's formation. She kept the bathroom occupied for an indefinitely longer time and every day drew a new LOC towards my side of the living room, curtailing my surface area. In short, she behaved like Pakistan. I was the stereotypical India. I didn't say anything. I didn't reply with loud music. I didn't take any revenge. I was irritated and kept my irritation to myself. I just stopped playing ice breaker games with her in class. Isn't that how India reacts to notorious Pakistan – stops playing cricket?

On the other hand, Tanishq and I took our relationship to the cellular level. We continuously chatted on Skype, and messaged each other back and forth. The time difference was challenging, but I managed it well. The wi-fi connection became a loyal companion. One of our duties was to wake each other up in the morning. My morning meant her evening and vice versa. I told her about my residence-mate being a girl and she was mad at me. Like any other girlfriend, she became insecure, but I told her my equation with my neighbour and she was relieved.

In a month, the neighbor and her eating into my space had gone beyond control. So I called my father for some wisdom.

Whenever I felt depressed. I called him and he was an expert to recognize when I was feeling low. So after the initial questions and pleasantries, I came to the point.

"I cannot get along with my roommate," I said.

"Why so?"

"I don't like her."

"Why don't you like her?"

"Because she is a Pakistani."

"Is that a reason to dislike someone?" he asked.

"Don't you think it is more than just a reason? Pakistanis are bad. They attack our country. They kill our soldiers," I vented out my anger against our neighbouring country.

"Did your roommate ever attack our country? Did she ever kill anyone?"

"No, but their people do."

"Don't judge people by their nationality or race. You are not in India anymore. You will meet people from all over the world. We know about Pakistan what our media shows us. We are aware of only those Pakistanis who throw bombs in our country. Not everyone is the same. There are good Pakistanis and there are bad Indians. Don't hate her for what her people did."

"But she gets on my nerves."

"That is because you made her hate you. Do I need to remind you why? Hatred always beacons hatred, my son. Be nice to her. You are probably the first Indian she has ever met. It is from you and your behaviour how she will judge all Indians. If you be nice to her, she will take a good image of India to her homeland. She will talk about you in her country and that will change the perspective of many other Pakistanis. You represent India, my son. Make sure you represent it well."

His words inspired me and as he hung up the phone, my chest broadened with pride and confidence. I felt proud of being an Indian. My perspective towards Pakistan and Pakistanis changed. I slid sorry cards under Madiha's door. I gave a the major portion of the disputed refrigerator to her and also resumed interaction with her during ice-breaker sessions. She didn't forgive me, but turned down the volume of the age-old Pakistani folk songs. In a few days, she rubbed off the LOC. It appeared to me that two nations were becoming one. But there was a long way to go.

Time-Zoned

Once I adapted myself in the foreign country, I got back to my routine job – the job of being a boyfriend. The long distance relationship was most endorsed by video calls on Skype. We ate together, we watched movies together and we shared our experiences, but everything happened in front of the webcam. The distance of twelve thousand kilometers was very well tackled by a 3.2 megapixel camera.

The only challenge we faced was the difference of ten-and-a-half hours. Her mornings were my evenings and vice versa. When I had time in the evening, she was mostly busy in college, and when she got home and had time, I was generally either attending lectures or was at the clinic. To acclimatize myself to this massive time difference, I stayed up late till 3 a.m. That was the only time when we both were free. It was a most convenient time except that it kept me away from my sleep. I forced myself to stay up late so that I could continue our love saga. After a hectic day at the university, it was tough for me to keep my eyes open. I drank numerous cups of tea to support my mechanism. Never once did I feel that I was forcing myself to stay awake. Once she smiled on that laptop screen, I felt energized.

To compensate for that lost sleep, I took naps between lectures. The micro naps were not enough to recharge my cells, so I learned to lean on the shoulders of my class mates. Sometimes they tossed me away from their shoulders and sometimes they nudged me hard to wake me up. I lived in a world of illusion. The days were the new nights for me, but due to the strict university rules, I could not miss lectures or labs.

In a semi-circular lecture theater, I regularly sat on the extreme left corner to prevent being spotted. Madiha usually sat right in front of me. She noticed me sleeping in a lecture. I fell on the table in front and the soft thud caught her attention. She turned around and found me snoozing. She knocked my head with her knuckles to wake me up. The professor was not very nice with undisciplined students. Had he caught me napping in the middle of the lecture, he would have kicked me out. To save me from getting kicked out, Madiha adjusted herself in a way that I safely hid behind her back. Her help allowed me to nap safely.

After the lecture and few minutes of safe napping, my seat-mate Ming told me what had happened.

"That girl in front of you saved your life," Ming said in a thick Chinese accent.

That night I sat in my LOC-free living room and waited for her to come out of her room. I wanted to thank her. She didn't step out. I eavesdrop at her door and heard her sobbing. I wanted to knock on the door, but resisted. She was crying inside and I left her on her own.

That me wonder whether something terrible was going on in her life. She felt homesick or maybe she missed someone. She didn't have any friends in the residence or university. Ignoring her completely, I went back to my cellular conversations with Tanishq. I talked to her about Madiha and noticed that every time I brought up her name, Tanishq raised her eyebrows.

"Why do you have to talk about her all the time?" Tanishq yelled from the laptop.

"I talked about her today for the first time."

"This is not the first time. And moreover, you eavesdropped on a girl. How immature is that?"

"I wanted to say thank you to her. She saved my life in class today. It doesn't hurt to say thanks."

"You don't want to thank her; you are looking for an excuse to talk to her."

"Why would I look for an excuse? It is basic courtesy to say thanks."

"For you, the basic courtesy is to hit on a girl. Don't lie to me."

"Where is this conversation going? I told you I heard a girl crying and why do you have to make a big issue out of it?"

"I am making a big issue out of it?" Tanishq yelled. "Why don't you tell me the truth that you don't need me anymore." She snapped her laptop screen over the keyboard, automatically disconnecting my call. That is when I realized that why long distance relationships are blamed for misunderstandings. The insecurities grow as time passes by. The patience levels go down. We fought over small issues. Skyrocketing mountains were fabricated over a mole hill.

I swallowed my ego and tried to video call her again. There was no reply.

The clock showed 3 a.m. I had a lab at 9:30 a.m. That meant I had hardly five hours to sleep. I left her messages apologizing and begging to talk to me. After calling her numerous times and shooting fifty something messages, I gave up and decided to sleep. I sent one last message to her before snoozing off to bed. It was a good night message.

I slipped my head under my quilt and was on my way to the dreamland. I was so tired that had I closed my eyes for three seconds, I would have been dead asleep. Before the third second, my cellphone beeped. I was forced to peek into my inbox.

A message from Tanishq that read, "*How can you sleep after disturbing someone else's sleep?*"

I called her again and this time, she picked up the phone. I begged again and she listened to my plea. After an hour long conversation, I succeeded in making her laugh. She forgave me for the crime I didn't commit. She was happy. She sent me virtual cellular kisses.

"Abby, I have to go to the market. You should sleep now," she said.

I sacrificed my sleep and she didn't appreciate that at all. I was allowed to sleep because she had to go to the market.

"Yes, I think so. You have a great day ahead. I will go to sleep now," I said without any complaints.

I peacefully ended the call. I looked at my bed. The bedsheet was neatly creased as it had been unbothered for the last few days. The pillow teased me. I moved my eyes towards the window. There was no more darkness outside. The darkest thing I saw was under my eyes. Some people call them dark circles. I call them signs to prove that you own a tantrum throwing girlfriend. Rather, she owned you.

My happiness was yet to rise but the sun already had. Birds chirped and brought themselves back to business. A few fitness freaks were in the park, jogging their way to the gym. The night security patrol team was signing off duty. This was the series of events in that one minute that convinced me I had spent the whole night without sleep. On one side of the window, there was my cozy bed that invited me to sleep; and on the other side was the university building that ordered me to stay awake. I was tired. My fatigued muscles lost all the power. The eyelids became the heaviest part of the body. Holding them open was a tough task. I allowed the heaviest part to shut down and laid myself a hundred and eighty degrees flat on the bed. I was blessed with one hour of sleep. I took a cold water shower to stay alert all day. It was the first day in the forensics laboratory. We were supposed to learn how to dissect the jaw bone of a cadaver. I reached the laboratory on time.

The forensics lab was one of the most interesting departments of the university. Here, the dead people were in the service of living ones. They were supposed to be dissected by future forensic odontologists.

Very soon, a cadaver was brought on a stretcher and was placed on the dissection table. For starters, dissecting cadavers is not an easy job. To do so, one has to keep their hearts aside. People in the forensics department were deemed heartless human beings for the same reason. They were short tempered, brutal and accepted zero error from a student. The department was led by Dr Douglas Banks, one of the pioneers in Forensics in North America. He was a huge Afro-American man with a tough voice. Dr Banks had this monstrous image amongst the Forensic students. He expected everyone to be on time, come prepared and stay focussed in the class. He entered the laboratory and his black color absorbed the light of the room. Then he opened his mouth and his shining white teeth reflected some light.

"Good morning class. I am Professor Banks and you can call me…," he took a beat, "…well, no one calls me anything but Professor Banks. This week I will teach you cranial, mandibular and arch morphology. You should dream about nothing but these three topics. Dream about them or you will be terrified by nightmares of a six feet five inches man."

After his terrifying speech, he handed the department rulebook to each student and took the podium once again.

"It is a two-page rulebook and I recommend you don't waste time in reading this. I will save you some time by telling you one simple rule. The only one thing that you can do in this lab without my permission is breathe. For everything else – ask. Tear the rulebook and come to the front."

We surrounded Professor Banks around the cadaver. He held the scalpel and brutally chopped the already dead body. He clearly explained the basics and divided students into groups of three to practically play with the cadaver. I was grouped with Madiha and Ming. We wore masks and gloves and waited for our turn. I continuously yawned to keep my brain active and strict instructions said I was allowed to only breathe. Yawning wasn't allowed. To commit this restricted act, I hid behind Ming.

"Stop it. Yawning is contagious. You are spreading lethargy," Ming whispered in my ears.

"I am so..rr..ry…" I said while yawning again.

Madiha gave me her trademark cold look and stood away from me. I desperately waited for the lab to end. I looked at the huge wall clock and second's hand crawled at snail's pace. I wanted to run to my room to get some sleep. I already made excuses in my mind that I was going to use to avoid late night conversations with Tanishq.

The scalpel blades moved to our group. I, Madiha and Ming moved towards the dissection table. I was supposed to participate in the group learning session, but my sleep deprived eyes focussed on the cadaver. Ming was right when he said yawning is contagious. Yawning is contagious and so is to see someone sleep. I looked at the closed eyes of the cadaver and felt jealous. The body resting in peace attracted my attention.

Ming read out lines from the book while Madiha demonstrated. She asked us to focus simultaneously on her hands and the cadaver. I partially followed her instructions and focussed only on the latter half – a body resting in peace. The eyelids got some weight to them and it felt like an overpowered gravitational force was pulling them. My ear drums got numb and the thick Chinese accent sounded like a stuck cassette in a stereo. The head tilted and knees started to bend. The brain entered a power saving mode as most of the organs switched off. The knees bent completely and my head fell on the plank over the dissection table. I tried to force open my eyes, but all attempts went in vain. The background sounds disappeared slowly and this followed a moment of silence. I felt like a mountaineer who had worked hard to climb the peaks of the Himalayas and had finally reached there. I was on top of the mountain and peacefully closed my eyes to feel the cold breeze. It was so peaceful. Suddenly, there was a huge animal yelling very loudly. He was so loud that I lost my balance and slipped down the mountain.

It was Professor Banks who banged his hand on the dissection table. The phenomenon reversed. Gravity didn't work on my eyelids anymore as my eyes were wide awake. The brain switched from the power saving mode to the emergency alert mode. He looked into my eyes. The mountaineer within me was on the ground. I was yet to diagnose what all damage had been done.

He came closer to me. I had to tilt my head backwards to look into his eyes. Now he seemed like the African version of Saabu – the sidekick of Chacha Chaudhary. I thought he would lift me with my collar and kick me out of the department. He tilted towards me and I bent in the opposite direction. From the position I was, I could see his huge nostrils. They were so huge that if he inhaled deeply, I would be vacuumed inside his nose in no time.

"What are you – a necrophiliac? Sleeping beside a dead body, next thing you want to make out with it. Is that the reason you came here to study forensics?"

He totally got the wrong idea. In normal circumstances, I would have tried to give an explanation, but here I knew I had committed a big mistake and decided to stay mum.

"Get out!" the big black tiger roared.

Fortunately, I left the department on my feet and not on a stretcher.

I had hardly slept for ten seconds but those ten seconds were reported to the authorities and it was considered a breach of the code of conduct. I was suspended from the department for two days. The university had a unique system of writing off a student. Any misconduct gave us a yellow sheet and for every yellow sheet, ten percent marks were deducted from the final score. Apart from two days of exile, my ten seconds won me one yellow sheet. Academically it was a black mark, but I utilized these two days exclusively to sleep.

I slept throughout the day and in the evening, someone knocked my door. I was in deep sleep and drooling saliva was the proof of a sound sleep. The knocking continued. Half asleep, I wiped the saliva and opened the door. It was Madiha holding two cups in her hand.

"Tea," she said as she offered me one of the cups.

I blinked my eyes repeatedly to make sure it was happening for real.

"You are not dreaming. It is me and I brought you some tea," she said.

"Thanks," I said holding the cup in my hands.

"Would you like to join me in the living room?"

"Sure. Let me wear a sweater. It is cold."

"I will wait."

I pulled over a sweater and sat on the couch beside her.

"I feel bad about what happened," she said, sipping tea from her mug.

"What happened?" I asked surprised.

"About what happened to you in the class, dumbo."

"Oh! Yes, I am sorry. I had a long sleep," the dumbo said relaxing on the couch.

"I can see that. Have some tea and wake up," she said passing me my cup.

"Thanks, but what happened when he kicked me out?"

"He was mad at the whole class and he was this close to take away our only right to breathe. I think we have to ask him to breathe too."

"I am sorry you had to..."

"Feel sorry for yourself. You are ruining your career."

"I couldn't sleep last night. I was studying for today's class," I said cunningly, sipping tea from my cup.

"Before lying, knock on the walls of your room. The walls here are not made of concrete. They are made of wood so thin that I can hear everything through them."

"What?" I said, shocked. I knocked the wall behind me and the woody resonance confirmed Madiha's point.

I felt embarrassed to have lied in front of her.

"What did you hear anyway?" I wanted to check.

"I cannot hear anything clearly, but I can hear enough to presume someone is living their life inside a phone."

"Same with me. I cannot hear many things clearly, but I can hear enough to presume someone cries a lot."

We both smiled at each other and then talked for hours. This was the first time we sat together and laughed about my stupidities. I told her about Tanishq and all the crazy stories from India. She nicknamed me Dumbo for my craziness.

"She better stay in your life. Got you kicked out of a job, tossed out of the apartment, and now almost molested in the department. I hope she appreciates that," Madiha said.

"I didn't tell her about today's incident. She would stop talking to me to save me the trouble. I love her a lot and all these things don't matter to me."

"Wow… Romeo! You are too nice to her. Be careful. Nice men don't have much luck with ladies."

She reminded me of Sattu. She had stated the same theory about nice men.

"You believe nice men finish last?" I asked.

"One hundred percent. Girls don't like someone who is nice to them. There is no challenge in that. Everyone loves challenge, as it gives a sense of victory. Girls like the challenge to win over other girls. If they know their man is not even looking at anyone else, whom will they defeat?"

"I will prove that theory wrong. Tanishq's sense of victory comes from the fact that her man is loyal to her. I will make her feel proud rather than making her jealous."

"That means she is never jealous of any other girl."

She had me wondering. I got tongue-tied as I had nothing to support my argument. Tanishq was very insecure. I started to doubt my relationship.

Seeing me numb, Madiha started laughing.

"Girls are complicated, Dumbo. Understanding them is beyond your limit," she said matter of factly.

"Enough of my story," I said, "now you tell me what makes you cry every night?"

Her laughter came to an end. She stood up saying she had to wash the dishes. I made her stay and forced her to tell me her sobbing-worthy secret.

"My life is complicated enough. My parents didn't want me to come here. They wanted me to get married. They found a guy for me. I wanted to escape marriage so I came here. They sent me but only after I got engaged to him."

"You are engaged? You are so young."

She nodded.

"That is the only drawback of my country. The daughter is a burden and parents want to get rid of them as soon as possible."

"It is the same in my country too. Why do you cry, though? You are safe here and two years of education is left. Who knows what will happen after two years."

"My fiancé wants to come here too. He wants to stay with me here in Canada."

"You don't like him?"

"I don't know him…how can I like him?"

"Maybe he is the right guy. You never know."

"Do I look like I will marry someone? I came to this university to follow my dreams not to marry some idiot."

"Why are you so paranoid about marriage?" I couldn't fathom.

"I have nothing against marriages, but I want to marry someone I love. Right now I have other important things to focus on. I have to establish myself as a successful forensic odontologist in Canada. After that I will think of falling in love."

"You don't think and fall in love. You simply fall in love."

"Romeo, what world are you living in?"

We talked for hours that night. She instructed me not to tell Tanishq about our conversations. I followed her instructions and lied to Tanishq. I didn't mention her name even once and Tanishq was more than happy.

The situation in my residence apartment was quite ironic. I had to force Tanishq to talk to me every night whereas Madiha was forced to talk to her fiancé. In a few days, we had become good friends. She reminded me of Sattu, except she was very beautiful and had a little less dirty mind than him. We started studying together. Once in a while, we cooked for each other. She learnt some vegetarian recipes from her mom so that she could cook for me.

Insecure

Madiha helped me in reforming my relationship. She continuously advised me what to do and what no to do, when to say and when not to say. She helped me understand girlfriend psychology. She was the female version of Sattu. She was skeptical about love, but she wanted me to live life for myself and explore the opportunities around me rather than dating a laptop screen. We started to go out and drink on weekends. I found a perfect friend in her.

Meanwhile in India, Tanishq finished her internship and took some time off from work. That provided her with all the time in the world. She woke up without the assistance of an alarm. She waited to get a field job and in the meantime, was a full-time girlfriend. She called anytime as per her convenience. She called me when she missed me, which was usually every hour.

"Hey Abby, I miss you," she said, with all the excitement.

"I am in the middle of a lecture. I will call you later," I said with half of my mouth open.

She called me in the evening.

"Hey Abby, I miss you," she said.

"I miss you too. I am studying for my test tomorrow. I will call you later."

She called me in the middle of the night.

"Hey Abby, I miss you."

"I miss you too," I said followed by a yawn.

"Oh, you were sleeping. Sorry, I didn't check the Canadian time."

But she didn't hang up after that. She continued talking while I lay down with cellphone placed over my ear. I hummed every time she asked me to agree on something.

By the end of the semester, I was kept busy with assignments, tests and my journals. She needed attention, while I struggled to keep pace with my academic endeavours.

Sometimes Madiha helped me with my homework while I spent time talking with Tanishq. I missed Tanishq equally but Professor Banks had an eye on me and that added to my struggle of getting good grades.

"Why don't you tell her to take a break?" Madiha suggested.

"I cannot take a break. I love her a lot," I replied.

"If Banks asks you why you didn't do your homework, give him the same answer."

"Is his homework due tomorrow?"

"Yes, sir."

"Madiha, my sweet Pakistani friend…"

"Stop it right there," she shouted, interrupting me in between.

She knew my flattering her with my sweetness only meant two things – Either I wanted her to make tea for me or I wanted her to do my assignment. She was not that naive to fall for my sweetness. Most of the times I had to order a pizza for her in exchange for her academic services or I had to buy alcohol to support her weekend entertainment.

One-fourth of my scholarship money was going as a bribe to get my homework up to date, but in turn, I got time to engage myself in sweet talk with my girlfriend.

We both won equal amount of scholarship, but since India's economy was stronger than Pakistan's, the conversion rate made my scholarship seem more than hers. She balanced the difference by looting me. I didn't mind that either. Her friendship was worth more than that extra scholarship that I gave away.

I narrowly escaped from the claws of Professor Banks. I blemished my academic report for my love life. I passed the first semester but the second semester came with some more challenges.

In the second semester, we were assigned clinical work. I was posted at the Dental OPD. Other challenges included entertaining a full-time girlfriend. The first thing that Tanishq did after waking up was to make a call. She had a belief that her day went marvellously if she listened to my voice in the morning. To make her day marvellous, I had to pick up her phone and say hello every day, irrespective of how busy I was. For her it was romantic; but for me, it was a dare. By the time she desired to listen to the lucky charm voice, that voice reached an area where the voice had to be managed, words had to be limited and desires had to be controlled – the Dental OPD. Ignoring the strict rules of OPD, I managed to talk to her for a minute. That's true love… forces you to do all the acts of bravery. There was another reason for showing this act of bravery. Not attending her calls meant inviting plenty of such calls, all crying to be answered, which in turn was followed by her tears. If those were left unanswered as well, the inbox was 'AK forty seven' with a dozen of *you don't love me anymore* messages. To avoid those cellular dangers, I took the call at once, said good morning, love you, take care and good bye – all in a span of less than a minute. I learnt some serious time management.

For her, this one minute of auspiciousness was more than enough to make her day. For me, this one minute was more than enough to prove my heroics.

A young female patient was sitting on the dental chair while I was all set to examine her. I was all geared up with safety glasses, mouth mask and blue nitrile gloves. My phone vibrated in my scrub pocket. The situation wasn't apt to receive a call as my fingers were shielded with contaminated nitrile gloves. I decided to postpone the act of courage till the time those gloves were on. The phone vibrated again… and again… and again. The young female patient heard the vibration.

"You can take the call. I can wait," she said.

"It is my routine alarm. It can wait," the sincere dental student said.

"Alarm at this time? You wake up in the evening?" she said, looking at her wrist watch.

"It is morning in India. My girlfriend wakes up at this time. She believes talking to me in the morning makes her day," I replied.

"That is so sweet. Pick it up and make her day. Pick it up," she insisted.

"It is almost illegal to use cellphones inside the OPD."

"This dental chair is hidden behind the pillar. No one will notice you. I will keep an eye."

Provoked by continuous vibration and inspired by the young female patient, I took the risk of pressing the green button on the keypad.

My shoulder was given the responsibility to hold the cellphone whereas the hands held the instruments used to diagnose a patient. I was digging the patient's enamel and listening to Tanishq at the same time. What a multitasker! A boyfriend and a dental student were simultaneously at work.

"Hello," the boyfriend said as the dental student dug the enamel.

The digging of enamel led to some discomfort to the patient and she screamed. I focussed on the patient, totally ignoring Tanishq.

"Let me do this," I said.

"It hurts," the patient replied.

"Don't close. Keep it open for me."

"Ouch. I cannot. It hurts a lot."

"Let me insert it once again," I said putting the instrument over her tooth.

"Ouch. Slowly please."

"Maybe it's because it is your first time. It hurts initially. It will be comfortable thereafter."

"Okay. But please go slow."

"Here I go. Slowly and slowly…"

"Aaah… aaah.…" The patient moaned as I removed decayed enamel with an explorer.

All this time, the phone was between my shoulders and ear and Tanishq was online.

"Abby!" Tanishq screamed over the phone, loud enough to numb my ears.

The loyal boyfriend was brought back to business as the girlfriend was too loud.

"Hey, I am so sorry. I was busy," I said on the cellphone.

"What the hell is going on there? Where are you?" she shouted again.

"I am in the OPD with my patient."

"Shut up! Don't lie to me."

"Lie! Why would I lie?"

She was convinced that I was lying. I scratched my brain and realized how my conversation could have been misinterpreted by an insecure girlfriend.

"Let me do this," Abby said to the beautiful girl, or let's say the bitch.

"It hurts," the bitch replied.

"Don't close. Keep it open for me." Abby said as he jumped over her again.

"Ouch. I cannot. It hurts a lot," the bitch repelled closing her legs.

"Let me insert it once," Abby said as he gently spread her legs.

"Ouch. Slowly please," the bitch said surrendering herself to Abby.

"Maybe it's because it is your first time. It hurts initially. It will be comfortable thereafter," Abby said as he dipped his beak into the bitch.

"Okay. But please go slow," the bitch commanded.

"Here I go. Slowly and slowly…" Abby said following the command.

"Aaah… aaah…" the bitch moaned in pleasure.

Oh god! "Trust me, I am in the OPD, treating a patient," I said.

"Treating a patient without clothes on your body?"

"What? Without clothes?"

"Don't lie to me. You are pounding a girl and she is in pain."

"What!" I said as I excused myself and left the patient unattended. "I got it. I wasn't asking her to open her clothes. I asked her to open her mouth. I was inserting the dental instruments, not my instrument."

"Oh god," she sighed. "I am so sorry."

"Use some logic. Why would I pick up your call if I am in the middle of pounding someone?" I said, in an attempt to make her laugh.

"That means there are chances that you can do it with some other girl?" she said, regaining firmness in her voice.

"No, I was just giving you an example."

"That was not an example. That was a desire."

"Flabby please," I scoffed, "not again."

"Why do you even talk to me when you don't want to?"

"I am not in a mood for another argument. This is not the right time and this is definitely not the right place."

"Had the place been right, you would fight, right?"

I banged the edge of the cellphone on my head to show my frustration.

"Can you share what important discussion is going on?" A very pleasurable voice interrupted the argument. Professor Dr Mary Yeomans.

I looked at Dr Yeomans. She was certainly not in a mood to settle the matter easily.

The call timer was still on.

"Answer me... Answer me..." Tanishq shouted from the other side, loud enough to make Dr Yeomans stare at the cellphone.

"Answer me first," Dr Yeomans repeated the words coming out of cellphone.

I pressed the red button, ending the timer.

"Carrying a cellphone in the department, number one; talking on the cellphone inside the department, number two; handling a contaminated object with sterile gloves, number three; and leaving the patient unattended, number four." Dr Yeomans announced the possible charges that could be laid on me. I imagined the possible outcomes: kicked out, number one; yellow sheet, number two; suspension, number three; and failed, number four.

My center of worry shifted from my falling love story to my falling career. Madiha always referred to my cellphone as the origin of all the tension. Dr Yeomans gave it a new name – a contaminated object. Very true. It had all the powers to contaminate a sincere student's report card.

"Give me your cellphone," Dr Yeomans ordered, placing a paper towel over her hands.

To save myself from any further charges, I placed the contaminated object over the paper towel. She wrapped the cellphone in the paper towel.

"Can you tell me who was on the other side?" Dr Yeomans asked making the battle personal.

I bowed my head with shame and stayed mute.

"Who was on the other side?" she repeated.

Before I could answer that question, my cellphone vibrated with a notification of one message received. She unwrapped the paper towel to look at the screen. Though these messages are considered personal, but if a curious teacher caught you red-handed, the personal entity is publicized. The curious teacher opened the message and the other side was revealed.

Reading the message Dr Yeomans' questions converted into an order.

"Wrap up the patient and come to my chamber."

I followed her commands and entered her chamber. I stood still as three professors discussed the punishment for me. I felt like I was being court-martialled. All the respect that I had earned so far for being a good student was about to fade away with this trial. After waiting there for around half an hour, Dr Yeomans read the trial.

"What you did today was a grade three breach in the code of conduct. With that being said, you will be written up with two yellow sheets, which mean an automatic twenty percent deduction from your final clinical grades. Seeing that the passing limit is seventy percent from here, you don't have much to lose. Make sure you work really hard to see yourself in the next semester."

I stood shocked. I started to do the maths about how to save myself from failing this semester. She ordered me to grab my contaminated cellphone from her table. As I moved to her table, it vibrated again. The three professors looked at the cellphone all at the same time.

"This is the first time in the history of the university that a scholarship awardee international student has received two yellow sheets simultaneously. Till now only one international student has failed the clinics. I don't want you to be the second one. Technically this contempt calls for a much rigorous action, but you are an international student. We consider the fact that you face cultural shock and homesickness. Hence this leniency is being granted to you. International students work very hard to reach here. Don't ruin that hard work over a meaningless issue. The department is confiscating your cellphone for a day. I hope you can think of your career better without a mobile device."

Terrified by the trial, I reached my residence. The news of my indiscipline spread like fire in dry grass.

"How irresponsible was that?" Madiha said as she pulled my ears.

"Stop it please, I have had enough for today," I said, throwing her hands away from my ears.

"Dude, you don't understand this. You have created history."

"I know. What do you want me to do? Celebrate this?" I yelled at Madiha.

She saw me losing my temper for the first time. I didn't like that either. She walked out of my room. I chased her and apologized for my behaviour.

"I am sorry. I guess I am too damn scared of failing," I said joining my hands.

"Why did you come here?"

"To say sorry."

"No Dumbo, why did you come to Canada?"

"I don't know."

"Then figure out. You beat thousands of other students who could have died to get admission in this university. Don't do this injustice to them. You don't realise how blessed you are to be here. Utilize this in building your career. Don't waste it over some stupid chick."

Madiha said some mean things about Tanishq. I didn't interrupt her and let her say what she felt about her. She was mad at Tanishq more than me. She warned me to stay away from my girlfriend if I wanted to pass the semester. She also refused to do my homework and instead asked me to cut down my late night video chats. Madiha cared for me more than anyone else and obeying her appeared to be the only way to save the semester.

After reinstating the possession of my cellphone I decided to discuss the matter with Tanishq. Madiha strictly instructed me to be firm and clear and not emotional. To make sure I understood the instructions well, she sat in front of me.

"This is called Lahori jutti," she said, using her shoe as a weapon, "this is shaping careers of us Pakistanis since 1947. If you don't do as I said, this will take care of your career."

I nodded and made the call. I explained the severity of my case to Tanishq.

"Let's take a break. It is not working out anymore," Tanishq announced.

"Like a temporary break or a full break?" I asked.

"We will see. Let us stop talking for some time."

I hadn't expected that, but it made me sad. I was about to break down and apologize again but Madiha sat in front of me showing me, her career-reshaping shoe every time I was on the verge of a breakdown. She knew I didn't have the courage to take a break and that's what made her sit in front of me with a shoe in her hand while I was on the phone.

Tanishq said a final goodbye and asked me to contact her after my final exams. That meant we had to abstain from talking to each other for three months. It was going to be tough. She hung up and I cried.

Madiha laughed at me.

"Awwww… the sweet little girl is crying," she said, mocking my tears.

"Shut up! You cannot imagine how I am feeling right now."

"Yeah how can I imagine, I am not thirteen!"

She laughed at me again as I hid my face under the pillow.

I preferred my career over Tanishq. I wanted to work hard to stay in class. I didn't want to be the second international student to fail. I probably hurt Tanishq, but at that point, that seemed to be the most suitable step.

Break

"I am tired. Let us sleep now," I said stretching my arms.

"We have to finish this subject tonight," Madiha said bringing me back to attention.

After taking a break from the relationship, I was able to focus on academics. Madiha and I studied together and she was very strict about it. She had a set timetable and I had to catch up with her speed. For the first time in my academic career, I finished all the assignments days before the due date. I didn't leave exam preparations for the last day.

And for the first time, I stayed away from Tanishq. I missed her a lot, but the fear of failure was always at the back of my mind. As much as I wanted to pass the semester, I wanted her back in my life. I hoped the break brought the same epiphany in her too.

It had been almost eight months since I had left India and within this short period of time, a series of events took place. Keshu got married to his long-time girlfriend Ankita. Shardul's parents found a girl for him on an online matrimony website. He was a married man too. It is only when your best friends get married you realize that time flies by really fast. The only saving grace was my friend Sattu who was, luckily, skeptical about marriage. To my shock, I got the news that Sattu was getting married soon. The news was beyond my imagination. I had to call him to confirm.

"Hello," I said.

"My friend Nandu," he said all excited. I skipped formal talk and jumped to the main question.

"Is it true?" I said.

"Yes."

"How in the world is that even possible? How come you said yes to marriage?"

"You left me alone here. There was no one to corrupt me."

"Don't fool around with me. Tell me how that happened. Who is the girl?"

"She is also a dentist. Very beautiful, very nice and very naïve. Exactly the way I wanted."

"Do you love her?"

"Hell yeah, I do. How difficult is it for me to love someone?"

"That is true too. I am very happy for you, my friend."

"You cannot just say it. You have to prove it. I want you here for my wedding. Actually, I want you here before my wedding."

"That will be difficult."

"I am not taking no for an answer. It is during the summer break. I am sure you can spare two weeks for me."

"Irrespective of the season, it will be tough for me."

"Just because you are not with Tanishq doesn't mean you don't have any reason to come to India."

"What! Who told you that?"

"I saw it myself."

"You saw what?"

"I saw her with some other dude."

"What?" I shouted. "Where and with whom?"

"Calm down. Wait, are you guys still together?"

"You tell me first where you saw her."

"I saw her at a CP coffee shop with a guy. We talked for around ten minutes and she said you were too busy and that's why insisted on a break-up."

"It wasn't a break-up. It was a break."

"She took it very seriously. She has moved on."

"What the hell? Who was the dude? Do you know him?"

"He looked happy to me, so he certainly is not a dentist. She told me his name. I cannot remember."

"Did she say he was her boyfriend?"

"She didn't say that, but the way they were sipping coffee from the same mug made me think so."

"What was the name of that bastard?"

"I don't remember his name. I thought you guys mutually broke up. She looked very normal to me. You are overreacting."

"I am not overreacting. I asked her to take a break so that I can focus on my career. It was a temporary thing. Not a break-up."

"I am sorry."

"Why didn't you tell me before?"

"Dude, don't blame me. You are the one who's been avoiding me all this time. I thought you were busy with some firangi chicks."

I realized I was blaming him for all the wrong reasons. I calmed myself down.

"I am sorry. I will talk to you later."

"Okay, but please come to my wedding. I need you."

"I will see."

I hung up. I told Madiha about the instance.

"I knew that was going to happen," she said.

"It wasn't supposed to. I will call her and talk to her about it."

"What will you say?"

"I will tell her how much I love her."

"This is not love. This is your ego. You cannot see her with anyone else," she said casually.

"Why should I? She was supposed to be with me. I won't let her go."

"If you want to give it a try, go ahead. But let me tell you again, it is too late now. She must have moved on."

I called Tanishq. She ignored my calls and didn't reply to my messages. She kept on saying she was busy.

After a week, she picked up my phone.

"Hey, how are you?" she asked.

"I am good, how are you?"

"I am doing fine, thanks."

"Don't you miss me?"

"Why would I? You were the one who asked for a break."

"It was supposed to be a temporary thing."

"Whatever. I don't miss you anymore."

"Why would you? You have moved on. I didn't expect this from you."

"Didn't expect what?"

"… that you will have someone else in your life. And that too so soon."

"Who told you that?"

"Don't fool me now. I know everything about the one with whom you are hanging out nowadays."

"Oh, you might be talking about Karan. He is my childhood friend. We are not dating, we are just good friends."

"Don't give me that 'just good friends' theory. I know how good a friend he is."

Our conversation turned into an argument soon. I yelled at her and she backfired.

"Whatever he is to me, you shouldn't be concerned anymore. You are the one who is sitting miles away from me. What I am going through, you don't even realize. Did you ever care about me?"

"Didn't I? I have jeopardized my career for you. It is because of you that I was seen outside lecture halls when I should be inside. It is because of you that I am on the verge of failing this semester."

"Don't blame me for your weaknesses. If you cannot handle your studies, don't find someone to blame."

"I am not blaming you. I am telling you how much I cared."

"I don't care anymore."

"Where did I go wrong?"

"I don't know. I just cannot handle this anymore. I don't want a cellular relationship."

She snapped at me and it was very clear. She had moved on.

I cried again and Madiha teased me for being a thirteen-year-old girl.

"She wasn't right for you." Madiha advised, "Let her go."

"I love her," I said as I sobbed.

"Girls don't think like you. A happy long distance relationship is a myth. It needs trust from both ends."

"Am I not trustworthy?"

"Yes you are, but maybe she is not."

She wanted me to face the reality but my heart wasn't ready to believe it.

"You have been dumped. Can't you see that? She has moved on," she said, rubbing her hand on my shoulder.

"I cannot take this anymore," I said.

"You definitely can. Have some sleep for now. Don't shift your focus from school."

I went off to bed and tried my best to forget what had happened. But it was not easy. The next few days were busy in the department and the mid-term exams helped me divert my mind from the break-up.

Soon after the last mid-term exams, Madiha planned a rescue operation for my smile. She shortlisted the single girls with whom I had a chance to hook up.

"Stop doing this. I am not interested," I said ignoring her list.

"Best way to get over a girl is to get on a girl. If you know what I mean," she said winking at me.

"I don't want to get over Tanishq. I love her and so does she. Her brain is clouded because of this distance. I will go to India this summer and clear it all. Then we will be happily together ever after."

Madiha slapped me gently on the back of my head. "Your brain is more clouded than hers. Don't even think of going back to India."

I didn't say anything because what I was planning was very impractical. Firstly, going to India during summer would require lots of money to buy a plane ticket; and secondly, a summer break was for assignments. I stopped my almost impossible dream right there. I was left with the only option of looking at the list now.

We shortlisted three most attractive girls from Madiha's list who would be ready to hook up. She messaged all the three girls simultaneously from my phone and assured me one of them would be in my room by the weekend. She had the same remedy that Sattu had used for me to overcome my previous break up, except that she said that decently.

The overly desperate text conversations were effective over one of the three targeted girls – Danielle Gauthier, a Canadian French girl who had been very kind to me in past.

"This brunette is going to make you forget Tanishq," Madiha announced as she fixed my date with Danielle.

"Do you think so? It is just a date."

"It is not just a date. Take her to the Greek restaurant…"

"Greek restaurant?" I interrupted, "Why Greek? I don't like Greek."

"Now you do. I told her your favorite cuisine is also Greek."

"I don't like Greek food."

"Suck it up, Nandu. You will probably eat more than just Greek. You are going to eat Canadian-French for dessert," she said.

Madiha's humor never failed to make me laugh. She wanted me to end the date in my room and do stuff.

"How can I bring a girl in my room on the first date and do stuff?"

"This is North America and a girl going on a date knows that there are chances of ending it in a room. And for the second part of the question, I guess you watch enough of Sunny Leone so I shouldn't tell you how to do stuff."

"I... I... don't watch Sunny Leone," I said.

"Nandu, make sure you have headphones on before lying to a neighbour who is only a wooden wall away. Oh God, that woman screams a lot."

I was embarrassed for my not so secretive action. I went to my room to save myself from further embarrassment.

I went out with Danielle on a Saturday. We went to the Greek restaurant and over dinner, we talked a lot. She asked me about my past relationship and I told her about Tanishq. She asked me more about her and I wen on and on. Madiha hated me when I talked to her about Tanishq. Talking to Danielle about her was relaxing. She was really nice to talk to. After the dinner, I invited her over to my place. She agreed to the offer. We took a cab and came to my residence apartment. Madiha opened the door for us.

"How was it, guys?" Madiha asked with a mischievous smile on her face.

"It was good," Danielle replied with a smile.

"Don't you have to sleep, Madiha?" I asked, indicating to her to leave me alone.

She got the signal and yawned on cue.

"Yes, I am very sleepy. I should go to bed."

I took Danielle to my room and we chatted for an hour before we dimmed the lights. We sat on the bed and I made my move. Dim light, complete silence, empty bed and a beautiful white girl on the side – the situation was apt for making love. I tried my best to look into her eyes, but some invisible force stopped me.

"Is everything okay?" Danielle asked.

"Yes… yes," I replied, gulping water from the bottle.

I sat beside her again and held her hand. I pulled her closer to me. I aimed my lips towards her and I closed my eyes. All I could hear during my best-concentrated power was Tanishq chanting my name Abby, and the echo of that name. My lips stopped where they were and I opened my eyes.

"Give me a minute," I requested Danielle.

"That is perfectly fine," she replied.

"You look so beautiful, I want to make the most of this night," I said trying to put a cover over my anxiety.

She chuckled and got up from the bed. She moved towards the switch board and turned on the lights.

"Whom are you lying to? Yourself?"

"I am not lying. I haven't kissed anyone since a long time so I am a bit nervous."

"Whom did you kiss last and do you remember when and where it was?"

"Absolutely. I kissed Tanishq on the 21st of August at the airport, right before I boarded my flight. It was incredible."

"Enough," she said interrupting me in between. "You haven't forgotten that kiss yet."

"No, I have completely forgotten that kiss. It is just it was at a very awkward location, so I still remember that," I said once again, trying to cover the lie.

"Stop lying to yourself and to me. Since the time this date started, you are only talking about Tanishq. You were trying to teach me Hindi and the only Hindi word I learned and will remember is Tanishq. Maybe you didn't realize this, but you are not over her. I was happy to be your rebound. I don't expect much from you, but I guess you cannot even kiss me."

"I can. Not only kiss. I want to do more than that," I said winking at her.

"Get out of her before you get inside me." Danielle patted my cheek and left the room. I plummeted myself on the bed. Danielle was right.

Danielle probably messaged Madiha about what had happened. The next morning, Madiha knocked on the door. I opened the door and she smiled with a cup in her hand.

"Good morning," I said rubbing my eyes.

"Good morning," Madiha said passing a sarcastic smile. She tossed the water in the cup on my face.

"Ouch! What was that?" I shouted.

"That was water to wake you up, Dumbo."

She beat me up with her fists as I tried to defend myself.

"I hooked you up with a Canadian bomb and you ruined it for an Indian matchstick," she said as she continued beating me.

"Stop it!" I yelled pushing her hands away from me, "Stop it! Don't pretend to care for me. If you really care for me then bring Tanishq back in my life. Just go away and leave me alone!"

My voice shook Madiha. She looked at me shocked and scared. I slammed the door and latched it from inside. Then I slid along the wall and sat on the floor only to realize what I had done. I felt bad for yelling at my best friend. I was missing Tanishq and that made me do terrible things. It had made me short tempered. I wanted her back in my life.

I called her again and again, but she never replied. She sent me a message saying she had moved on and so should I. I wish I could tell her that even if I tried, I could not move on.

I wanted someone to talk to. I called up Sattu. I woke him up from the middle of his sleep.

"Hello," he said, "Nandu, is everything alright?"

"Nothing is alright. I miss Tanishq and she asked me to move on."

"I can understand that, my friend. What can we do now? Try some boobs I guess."

Doesn't matter what time it was or what situation he was in, this guy could talk about boobs. He gave the same speech on boobs and rejuvenation of manhood.

"I miss you," I said, smiling.

"I hope you are fine. I know people in Canada are very open-minded, but Nandu I haven't seen you like that. I like you only as a friend."

"Shut up! I miss you and all the good old days. I want to come back to India but I don't have the money."

"I wish you could come for my wedding."

"I wish I could, but I am really broke."

"Can I send you the plane tickets?"

"No, thanks. It is okay."

"Are you sure?"

"Positive. You tell me how did this happen? I want to know Sattu. How come a guy who loved exploring boobs is finally settling for one pair?"

"It just happened."

"It didn't just happen. You have to tell me how did you agree to marriage when you hated commitment?"

"No one hates commitment. Sometimes it is that we couldn't find the right person to commit to."

"Whom did you want to commit?"

"Remember the girl whom I called every time after getting drunk?"

"Are you getting married to her? Who is she?"

"I wish. She was my girlfriend in school. She was my first love. We broke up when I got admission into dental college. I didn't want the long distance crap. Plus, I saw more potential to date in a dental college. After dating a bunch of girls, I realized she was the one, but it was too late by then. She was gone. I tried to find her in other girls. I began to distract myself by sleeping around with other girls. Nothing helped. She moved on very soon and I was waiting for her. I didn't have the courage to call her when sober. Alcohol was my best excuse to call her. She was nice and entertained me, but one day I got the news that she was getting married. She asked me to stop calling. I was thrashed. I hated myself for letting her go."

"Wow!" I was left tongue-tied. Even in my weirdest dream, I could have never thought that Sattu could love someone. Bastard loved a girl madly since his high school days and corrupted everyone around him by making them skeptical about love.

He continued, "I used boobs to rejuvenate myself, but my friend, you know it doesn't matter how many boobs you fondle… ultimately there will be one girl you will love irrespective of her boob size or shape. You will chase her till there is hope."

"Why did you give up now?"

"She got married to a very nice guy. Maybe she deserved him."

"That means the hope died?"

"I will answer that later. It is two in the morning. I need to sleep."

"Good night."

"Good night, and if you don't want to cry in your life, don't let her go."

Sattu's confession made numerous shock waves run through my body. All these years I had seen him as the happiest man on earth. It was all a lie. He cried for a girl for so many years and never let it show on his face. He didn't want any of us to cry the same way. He had won my respect.

India Calling

I took Sattu's words too seriously. I didn't want to go through the period of repentance like he had. I decided to go back to India for the summer.

To do this, I had to earn some money to buy a plane ticket and to buy gifts for my friends. Second I had to convince Madiha to take care of my summer assignments. Apparently, the first step was easier than the second. I applied for part-time jobs and got one at the Tim Hortons, which is like the Starbucks of Canada. Getting hired by this café restaurant chain was not at all difficult.

"How will you manage the university schedule if you work?" Madiha asked when I told her I was going to work part time.

"I will do it. I am doing night shifts from 11 p.m. to 7 a.m. From there I will come to the residence, take a quick shower and go to class. Everything is well planned. I just have to cut on my sleep."

"When will you do your homework and when will you study?"

"The night shifts aren't busy. I will have plenty of time there to study, and for homework, we will do it in between classes. I calculated and found out we waste plenty of time sitting in the cafeteria. We have to manage that time properly."

"Why are you saying 'we'? I am not working at Tim Hortons. I can do my homework during the night."

"Please Madiha," I said joining my hands and bowing in front of her.

"Not anymore. This isn't the first semester anymore. This is very tough for me."

"Please. This is tough for me. I am going through a bad phase. I cannot concentrate on my studies till I don't find what is going on in Tanishq's mind. I have to go to India. and I need money."

"Okay fine. I will do it. You owe me big time, Nandu."

"I know Madiha. I would have died if you were not here."

In this emotional outflow, I hugged Madiha for the first time. I apologized for screaming at her.

"Have you ever loved someone?" I asked her, resting myself on her shoulder.

"Where is this coming from?" she said pulling away from me.

"It is coming from my curious mind. You only talked about the one whom you don't like. You never mentioned if you love someone."

She blushed and didn't reply. I insisted again and she shook her head. She made an excuse of making a phone call to her parents and left the conversation in between.

Madiha's sister called her almost every day from Lahore and I took the liberty to talk to her younger sister while Madiha was busy doing my homework. She had lifted the ban on Tanishq talks, so we now talked about it too. Her sister found it cute that I was working so hard to get Tanishq back into my life. Madiha had somehow developed a secret hatred for Tanishq. And why not? She was the one who had to tolerate all my crazy tantrums. She was the one whose workload augmented because of Tanishq. So much so, that she used to refer to her as a vamp.

Every day before leaving for work at eleven, I cooked food for Madiha to make sure she could do my homework uninterrupted.

Every day while returning at seven in the morning I brought food and tea for her from Tim Hortons and woke her up. This became our routine. She curtailed her personal time that she had sanctioned for calling her parents and with full dedication did my homework every day. That is when I talked to her sister while cooking for her. Her sister was the only person who said I was cute. Everyone else who knew about my story – which was almost everyone at my workplace – termed me crazy.

The legends of my crazy rudimentary love story were echoing in Sudbury, New Delhi, and even Lahore. I was able to garner sufficient money to buy a return ticket to India. I carefully planned my stay in India with expert opinion from Madiha. She wanted me to spend nothing more than two weeks. Unfortunately, I would miss Sattu's wedding as it coincided with my final exams. But he volunteered to lend me his place for my stay in New Delhi.

"You are newly married. Are you sure I can stay at your place?" I said to him.

"I live in a two-storeyed unit. You take the second floor. Just don't bring any girls over," he said.

"Not a problem. Thank you so much. I will see you soon."

Tickets: done. A place to stay: done. All I had to do now was call Tanishq and tell her about my endeavors. I called her.

"Hey Abby, how are you?" she said excitedly.

For a moment, I thought nothing had changed. It was exactly the same enthusiasm and same smile.

"Where have you been?" she asked.

As if she didn't know I was not her boyfriend anymore.

"I was busy with my school and my job," I replied.

"You have a job now?"

"It is a part-time job at a café."

"Oh, so you are a waiter now. That's what you studied dentistry for?"

Damn! I wanted to yell that it was for her that I was sweeping floors and washing dishes. But I had to calm myself down.

"It is a part-time job for some extra bucks."

"That is very strange. Three months ago you didn't have time for me and now you have enough to earn some extra bucks."

"It is not that I have time. I had to take some time out for this job."

"You could have done the same for me."

I was trapped by my own words. Now she wanted an explanation. Why could I find time for a job and not for her? Because a job had a particular time, a fixed schedule and it didn't get me kicked out of the class. My girlfriend had no schedule at all.

She began to rip off the old wound by blaming me for our break up. I didn't have the patience to listen to her. I intervened in between her blame game.

"I am coming to India next week," I said.

"Good for you."

I waited for her to say something else. She didn't.

"That is it? Good for you? That's all you have to say? Aren't you excited?"

"Please, Abby. Stop it. You know it and I know it. There is no point of hiding it now. I am seeing someone else."

"You could have waited for me."

"I did. I waited for you. But you were too late."

She hung up on me. I was left devastated. Madiha heard my conversations with Tanishq. She gave me the deadly look, betokening that I had made a big mistake. She didn't say anything. Her eyes said everything.

I had already booked the non-refundable tickets. That was the point of no return. My bags were packed. The only hurdle I had to jump was the last exam and one last assignment. Both the exam and the assignment due date were on the same day. And my flight was on the same night. A night before the final exam, I worked the night shift at Tim Hortons. That was my last day at work. I studied while working. Somehow I nailed the exam, but had not yet touched the massive assignment. Madiha was busy with her exams and assignments. After writing the exam, I had only three hours to finish my assignment and two hours to reach the airport. There was no way I could have finished the assignment.

"Please do me this last favour. Please do this assignment for me," I pleaded in front of her.

"I understand your condition, but it is a big assignment. It took me two days to do mine. How do you expect me to do yours in three hours?"

"Paraphrase whatever you have done. I don't care."

"It is a five page evidence-based research material. Everyone has to come up with a unique research topic. How do you want me to paraphrase mine?"

"I know you can come up with something. I want to go to India without any tension. I already have a big tension waiting up there. Let me focus on solving that. Please take care of this one."

I forced her to the level of irritation. She lost it at the end and said yes.

Ming came to my room to pick me up. He had a big book in his hand.

"What is that?" I asked, seeing the book in his hand.

"*Gray's Anatomy,*" Ming replied.

Gray's Anatomy is a textbook that is considered the Bible of anatomy. It had to be mandatorily swallowed to pass all the semesters.

"Exams are done. Why did you bring that book?" I asked.

"It is for you," Madiha said. "Put your hand on this book and take an oath."

"How old are you guys?" I said, "This is so crazy."

"This is crazy and what you do is totally fine?" Madiha said.

"This is for you, and more so, for us. We don't want you to bug us anymore with that one name," Ming said.

"Put your hand on the book," Madiha instructed.

"Okay fine," I said as I placed my hand on top of the mighty book.

"Now repeat after me," Madiha said.

Ming held the book for me and I put my right hand over the book.

"I do swear in the name of *Gray's Anatomy* that I will return from India with a smile," Madiha said.

"I, Nandu, do swear in the name of *Gray's Anatomy* that I will return from India with a smile," I said.

"I will never ever talk about Tanishq or any of the moments spent with her. I will never annoy anyone with all my 'If-I-was-with-Tanishq' fairy tales," Madiha said.

And I repeated the same.

"I will start staring at girls without comparing them with Tanishq. I will start dating girls without comparing their eyes, nose, hair, forehead, voice, or fragrance with that of Tanishq's."

"You guys are so demanding," I said pulling my hand away from the book.

"You want to know why we are demanding?" Madiha said grabbing my wrist and putting it back over the book. "Because you are so annoying. In the past one year, all this town is hearing is about Tanishq. All this town is experiencing is your idiotic non-reciprocating love for Tanishq. You have portrayed her as if she is actually an angel from Venus..."

"She *is* an angel from Venus," I intervened.

"Shut up! Don't interrupt and listen. Those who have never seen her are dying to see her. Guys want to see her because they are assuming she must be no less than some Miss Universe as she had prevented you from scoring chicks in this land of opportunities.

Girls of this town want to see her because they are wondering what's so special about her that you have refused to date any of them. Every time we set you up with a girl, you start complaining," Madiha said, ranting out her anger against Tanishq.

"Please, respect!"

"We will respect her if you come back as our friend Nandu. We want to see the same charming Nandu whom we met. Not a loser. There are a bunch of girls who are ready to fall for you. Give them a chance."

"I want only one girl to fall for me. I want only one girl to experience this charm. And you all know that."

"You are impossible!" Madiha screamed and pushed me out of the room. "Ming, throw him at the airport and make sure he never comes back."

Ming dropped me to the airport and after some time, I was off on a fifteen-day mission. On the plane, looking out of the window I planned the mission. I named it 'How to win Tanishq's heart- season 2'. I came up with many creative ideas and smiled.

After a seven hour long journey I reached London where the flight had to make a four-hour-long stay. I got off the plane and turned on the wi-fi on my phone. I messaged Madiha to enquire about my assignment. She replied that it had been successfully submitted. She didn't talk much after that. To kill time I chatted with Ming and he got all charged up at me.

Ming: *How could you be so selfish?*

Me: *What did I do? I paid you the gas money for the ride to the airport, right.*

Ming: *Not the money. How could you do this to Madiha?*

Me: *What did I do to her?*

Ming: *She got caught for plagiarism and got reported for academic dishonesty. She got a Dean Call and might fail the semester if found guilty.*

Dean Call or DC was the result of extreme level of academic misconduct. It might result in suspension, retention in the same semester and in worst cases, expulsion from the university.

Me: *WTF!!! How did this happen?*

Ming: *She precisely copied the same assignment and submitted it in your name. When Professor asked who copied from whom, she said she copied it from you. So you are safe, but she is in deep trouble. No student has ever came clear of DC.*

I couldn't believe she had done that for me. I was left dumbstruck. I messaged her, but she didn't reply. I never thought this would happen. Ming was right. I had been selfish. I wanted Tanishq and that had made me so selfish that I didn't care about people around me who really cared for me. My best friend who had stood by me during my worst phase. I had ruined her career.

I sat at the airport and certain memories came flashing back to me. I remembered the time I had yelled at her. I couldn't feel any worse. She cared for me beyond the farthest point. Who does that?

I had hated Madiha because she was a Pakistani, and today, what this Pakistani girl had done, I am sure even an Indian wouldn't have.

The public address speaker announced the departure of the flight and I boarded the plane. The plane flew towards my motherland. The next few hours, I stopped planning my mission and cursed myself for being so mean and selfish.

Five Days

Tortured with regret and filled with remorse, I reached India. As I stepped out of the airport, a thali waited for me. My parents had come to pick me up. It was a pleasure seeing them after almost a year. After the initial hugs and rituals, they drove me to my hometown Nainital where I spent the first ten days of my vacation. That left me with only five more days to accomplish my mission.

Without wasting any time, I travelled to Delhi. The same day, I met all three of my married friends. It was like a reunion. We went to our regular hangout spots and got drunk in our own Chana Chabena Dhaba. All the good old memories struck back, but I felt like I was drinking with some responsible grown-up men. All three of them discussed their work, and the likes and dislikes of their wives. I felt like the odd man out. Sometimes they also boasted how they were the lions of their house and dominated their wives. The transfiguration of a brave lion into a scary cat was only one phone call away. The three obedient husbands left at a decent time after receiving phone calls from their respective wives.

I went back to Sattu's place which was my planning headquarters. I called Tanishq to fix a meeting. She seemed pretty excited to meet me, but told me clearly that she was in love with someone else.

"I have moved on. I can meet you only if you promise to be a friend," she said on the phone.

"Sure, I have moved on too. I just got a few gifts for you, so let us meet somewhere."

I had to lie to her to convince her to meet me. That was the only way to get an affirmative answer from her. Luckily, she was on her summer break and with a few more lies, I was able to convince her to meet me on all five days.

Relationships are like skyscrapers on a plot. You start with building trust on a plot and that's when your skyscraper builds – brick by brick, cemented with trust and painted with compassion. It needs lots of determination, loyalty and patience. If the combination is right, you get a tall, strong and beautiful skyscraper that stays forever. Tanishq's heart had already been occupied by some other skyscraper. My skyscraper had been demolished, and to rebuild mine. I had to demolish this already existing tower. It was a long procedure but I had to accomplish this in five days. Feeding my determination with this architectural analogy, I commenced the mission.

DAY 1

I met her at her favorite Café Coffee Day. I went there an hour before the anticipated time of the meeting. It was my only chance to win her heart back and I didn't want to risk anything. I overestimated the traffic and left my place early. I kept our favorite corner reserved for us – the one by the window. She always sat facing the window so that she could keep an eye on the world. I sat with my back towards the window because I didn't care about the world and wanted to keep my eyes on her.

Tanishq entered the café an hour after the meeting time. She opened the door and I turned my back to look at her. The world stopped for me again. The people chatting around me seemed to pause. The barista holding the tray in her hand was on halt. I could only see Tanishq walking in slow motion, wearing a denim shirt and black aviator sunglasses. She walked towards me as her neatly made hair bounced. I fixed my eyes on her slow motion walk and that dropped my jaw. I got up from the chair and stood still as she moved towards me to hug me. She was like medicine to my heartache and solution to my restlessness. Medical science has termed this condition as euphoria, the exact feeling a normal individual gets after taking recreational drugs. And that is why people get addicted to these drugs, for the sake of euphoria. I didn't need a drug to feel that. I needed Tanishq. The euphoria wasn't long lasting as she softened the grip on my back.

"It is so good to see you again," she said as she took off her sunglasses.

I stood still for a bit. She snapped her fingers in front of my eyes. I blinked my eyes and came back the reality.

"Look at you," she said, "you look so different."

"In a good way?"

"Definitely in a good way. You look so muscular."

I don't know if that was true or not, but I felt like my chest pounded outwards and I felt pumped up. I sent some signals to my not so developed mini-biceps and they tried their best to bulge out of my t-shirt sleeves.

"Yes. I have been working out lately," I said, flexing my muscles.

"I can see that."

She ordered her favorite cappuccino and I ordered my tea. We talked a lot. We told each other how the past one year had been. Then we discussed a few common friends. She was the one who did most of the talking. I didn't care where her best friends were. I sat there wondering what made her so special. Her eyes revealed all the answers.

I couldn't believe that this was happening. To confirm that there was no screen in between, I touched her face quite a few times.

"Are you okay?" she asked every time I touched her.

"Yes," I replied. "I have been video chatting with you for a long time. It is hard to believe this is happening. I wanted to make sure there is no laptop screen in between."

"That's so cute," she said as she touched my face in the same manner.

"Wow! It is really you," she said as she pinched my nose.

Before I left, Madiha had given me instructions to control my desperation and not beg in front of Tanishq like a pet dog. But here I was.

"I love you Tanishq."

"What!" She spilled the coffee out of her mouth and sprayed everyone in a radius of two meters. I grabbed a napkin to wipe my face.

"I am so sorry," I said. "I tried my best but I cannot help it."

"You have to. I... I... don't...."

"Sssshhhh!" I said pressing my palm against her lips. "Don't say anything. I don't need an answer. I love you and I don't expect anything from you."

"I don't want to hurt you."

"Nothing much is left to get hurt."

"Abby..." she said, rolling her lower lip. That face is possibly the cutest look in the world. It never failed to make me smile. It continued its charm and I smiled.

"Why are you so cute?" I said putting a smile on my face.

She laughed and kept the same look for few more minutes. We chatted again and then went for a stroll. While walking along the massive white pillars of CP, she told me the most heartbreaking story. The story of her and her new 'just friend'.

"I was heartbroken at that time and so was Karan. We both were trying to overcome a break-up and somehow ended up meeting every day. And I don't know how it happened eventually," she said.

It felt like some invisible monster had drawn his hand through my mouth and squeezed my heart. I could feel the pain, right in my heart. I didn't say a word. I didn't ask too much about him.

"I think we should go home. I have to be home by six," she said.

I didn't want her to leave and could have insisted, but I needed some alone time to vent out the tears. We hugged a goodbye and planned to meet the next day at some other spot. She dropped me at Sattu's place and left.

I came to his guest room and locked myself inside before crying my heart out.

The whole night I was kept busy by Sattu and his wife. His wife wanted me to narrate his college stories. She put me in a dilemma. All the stories I had with Sattu had girls involved. To her, her husband was a very shy guy in college. I didn't want to wreck their forty-five-day old marriage. And I came up with how I met her husband Sattu, the only story without a girl. She laughed at the funny story but insisted I narrate some more. I had to edit all the stories that Sattu had with the girls, except I played the role of Sattu in the story and he was playing the nice guy Nandu. His wife enjoyed most of those reconstructed stories and pulled his cheeks for his cuteness in college. She also seemed a bit disappointed with me and probably warned her cute husband to stay away from me.

DAY 2

Tanishq came to pick me up in the morning. She drove us to the same highway where we had gone on our first night out. We stopped at the same dhaba where she had named me Abby. We had lunch there. She ordered the same mighty paratha to satisfy her

Punjabi appetite. Then we drove back to Gopu's tea stall. Gopu had grown up really fast. He had some facial hair now and his tea stall had expanded to accommodate chairs and tables. He recognized both of us and was elated to see us. After a small conversation with him, he made me my favorite tea. I looked at the same tree where Gopu had hooked Lord Shiva's poster. The photo was still there. I looked at the Lord's photo and prayed to him.

There was some miraculous connection between me and that specific poster. He listened to me really quick. As we waited for our tea, Tanishq got a call from Karan and she started to yell on the phone. Apparently, there was some tension going on between them. She looked disturbed while talking to him. I titled my head again to look at the poster.

"Thank you." I winked.

Tanishq hung up the phone.

"What's the matter, if you don't mind me asking?" I asked pretending I didn't care.

"He is annoying sometimes. He doesn't give me time. He always makes excuses, but has all time for his friends."

"Oh, he shouldn't lie to you," I showed fake empathy and added some fuel to speed up the fire.

"Exactly! That is what I said."

"It is a beautiful sunny day. He should spend time with you."

"He finds it too hot to go out. He is such a spoilt child. Instead stays at home and plays on his XBox."

"Wow! This is hot for him. If I had a girlfriend like you, I could even live on Mercury."

Tanishq smiled. "Stop it Abby. How much will you lie?"

She knew I was setting flames between them.

She didn't stop there and went on and on to vent her anger on Karan. I sat there as I dipped my Parle-G biscuit in the tea and nodded every time she asked me a closed-ended question.

Day two had been a success. I was able to make some impact. The foundation of her relationship with Karan had begun to rock. All I wanted to do was blow some air to cause a collapse. I had three more days to do so. The sun shone for me; all I had to do was make hay.

DAY 3

I planned to quake the base that had already been disturbed. I was confident that I would do it in the desired timel. But the day didn't start well.

At ten in the morning, Tanishq called me. "Hey, my car broke down. I am not sure if I can come out."

What perfect timing! "So what, let us use public transport today," I suggested.

"No. It is hot out there. Any vehicle without an AC would be inconvenient. Let us skip meeting today."

"No please don't. We can go somewhere close by."

"No, I don't want to be spotted with a guy near my house."

"Please, Flabby."

"Please, Abby."

She turned down the offer. My plans for building a monument had to be put on hold. I asked Sattu for his car, but the scared husband couldn't offer the vehicle his wife had brought as a wedding gift. I sat on his balcony to moan over a wasted day. I sipped on my morning tea as I looked at the road. I saw an auto-rickshaw driver arguing with a passenger. The topic of argument was definitely monetary. The fat lady passenger wanted to save some five odd rupees, I gathered. Soon, the neighbours came to aunty's rescue. The poor driver was surrounded by six middle-aged men who had their sleeves all rolled up. Already depressed by Tanishq's refusal to meet, the loud noise they made was exasperating. I went down with a five rupee note and gave it to the driver. Soon the wrangle came to an end. But the driver was a man of virtues. He accepted the money but handed that five rupee note to aunty.

"I think you need it more than me," the poor driver said.

Aunty was ashamed of her act and so were the other six unwanted men. They left and the show came to an end. The driver thanked me and returned my five rupee note.

"I didn't drive you around, sir. I cannot accept your money," he said.

People like him are very few. I wanted to help him. My mind got invigorated by his kindness and an idea popped where both of us could help each other.

"So Vishnu, how much do you make in one day?" I asked him as I read the name on his badge pinned to his chest.

"It mostly depends on the day, but this season, the maximum has been eight hundred, but two hundred goes in gas every day."

"I will pay you two thousand. I need you for a full day. I will pay for the gas too."

"That is sweet of you, but I am not a beggar. I work hard to earn money."

"You have to work harder than you think. That is why I am paying you a thousand bucks."

"What do I have to do?"

"You have to chauffeur me around the city."

"That is not hard work. That is what I do to earn money."

"Here is the catch, my friend. We have to pick up a girl from her place. She might throw some tantrums and be mad at me. In the process, she might yell at you too. Then she might agree to sit in the rickshaw, but will complain the whole time. You will have to bear all that. Two thousand one hundred bucks plus gas. My last offer."

"She cannot be worse than this fat lady. I am ready."

"Give me five minutes."

I went in to change and informed Tanishq I was coming, but didn't tell her I was coming in an auto-rickshaw.

On my way to her place, I bonded with Vishnu. He was a twenty-four-year-old from Bihar. He was thin and looked malnourished at first sight, but he was dressed well and had nicely combed hair. He told me he was a graduate in arts but could not find a job. Inside the rickshaw, he had a few stickers with funny one-liners and a woofered music system that played his favorite Bhojpuri songs.

We reached the shopping complex close to Tanishq's apartment building. She expected me to be in a four wheeler car, but it was a three-wheeler instead. She came all dressed up and called me.

"Abby, I cannot see a car. Where are you?" She said.

"See it carefully. It is right in front of the big water tank."

"I cannot see it. What color is it?"

"Green and yellow."

"No, I cannot. There is only an auto-rickshaw."

"Is it green and yellow in color?"

"Yes."

"Then that is the one."

She saw me waving at her from inside the auto-rickshaw. I got down welcoming her.

"Hello Your Highness," I greeted her as I got out of the rickshaw. "I brought the royal chariot for you. A three-wheeled automatic machine powered by a five horsepower engine propelled by eco-friendly compressed natural gas and highly equipped with world's most primitive and highly effective air-conditioner, i.e., cross ventilation. It will be chauffeured by Mr Vishnu. Vishnu say hi." Vishnu waved at her and she waved back at him awkwardly.

After the description of my royal chariot, I waited for Her Highness' reaction. I anticipated her to get mad, but surprisingly, she laughed. She found the gesture cute and sat beside me. Vishnu looked into the mirror and we made eye contact. I sighed with relief and he smiled. We went on a mini Delhi tour. We covered most of the famous monuments.

Wherever we went, Vishnu waited for us. We exchanged phone numbers and he was only an SMS away. Later that evening, we went to eat golgappas. Tanishq guided Vishnu to her favorite golgappa place. Within no time, she gulped quite a few of golgappas soaked in spicy water. I tried to compete with her, but could eat only half the amount.

As we walked through the narrow streets of crowded Old Delhi, a guy accidently elbowed her. He was a six-feet something, muscular young lad who had long bleached hair with a middle parting. He wore a very bright and tight t-shirt flaunting his muscles. The physical appearance made it evident he was a loafer.

"Ouch, you moron," Tanishq screamed at him.

"Attitude!" the guy retorted.

"Stay within your limits, you douchebag."

"You swear one more time and I will tell you who am I," the douchebag said, all charged up.

"Douchebag, douchebag, douchebag! I swore three times. Now tell me who you are," Tanishq teased him.

"Hey you," the douchebag turned towards me, "take your girl away. Teach her some manners."

I wasn't sure how to react as I wasn't programmed to respond to situations like these. A girl whom I loved was being aggravated by some douchebag and I stood mute. I felt dumb. I didn't have a violent bone in my body and she knew it very well. Neither did I possess muscles. I was also a few inches shorter than the violent douchebag. She veiled me behind her and took charge.

"Talk to me!" she whooped him.

They locked horns and the argument heated up. Words fired from both sides. I tried to pull Tanishq away and asked her to ignore him, but she was adamant to fight. Over the years, I had developed some non-violent techniques to deal with such situations. These techniques included humour and an even more efficient one –

fleeing. I was looking forward to the second option. I saw the auto-rickshaw waiting for us at a visible distance. I calculated the approximate time it would take me to reach that distance when I grab Tanishq's hand and run.

Before I could grab her hand, the douchebag grabbed her wrist. Tanishq was in pain and that was one thing that I couldn't tolerate. The fingers of my right hand folded into a fist. The blood boiled beyond its boiling point and the volcano exploded. I screamed at the top of my voice and lifted the anger-triggered fist towards his face. I punched his jaw with all my power. It was so powerful that we heard a bone cracking sound in the otherwise noisy streets. The douchebag lost his balance and plunged flat into the ground. Dust scattered a few inches over his body as he thudded on the ground.

Tanishq was so proud of me that she patted my back. As the volcano within me transformed into dormancy, I realized what I had done. I felt the pain in my fingers. I wasn't sure whether the bone cracking sound had originated from his jaw or whether I had fractured my phalanges. Tanishq jumped in the air out of joy and cheered me up. I didn't let the pain show on my face. She hugged me and teased the swooned douchebag.

"Tsk tsk tsk tsk tsk," Tanishq showed her pity.

He grunted in pain on the ground, but provoked by Tanishq, he regained his consciousness and tried to fight back for his ego. He tried his best to get on his feet.

"Come on Abby. Once more," she screamed.

She wanted me to punch him again, but I knew the volcano had cooled down. Now I had to use the conventional escape plans. Humour wouldn't work because the opponent's ego was wounded. I had to run. I grabbed Tanishq's wrist and before the douchebag could stand up on his feet, we ran from there. He was quick to chase us with that broken jaw. I indicated Vishnu to get into the auto-rickshaw and fly.

Tanishq hugged me out of excitement and then narrated the story of my heroics to Vishnu.

"My Abby is the strongest," she said.

I tried my best to control the pain. My fingers were swollen and I had to conceal them from being visible to Tanishq. My heart was still throbbing with fear, but I covered that too.

"Thank you, Abby. I never knew you could do that for me," she said as she got out of the auto-rickshaw.

I dropped her at her place and once she left, I moaned over the unbearable pain. I asked Vishnu to take me to a doctor. The doctor suggested a radiograph on my right hand. Luckily there was no sign of fracture. Certainly then, the douchebag had a broken jaw.

The whole day, Tanishq hadn't discussed anything about Karan. She didn't even look at her phone. As planned, I was able to shake the foundation. Not only that, with that punch, I demolished the skyscraper and I could see the multiple storeys collapsing. I went home to sleep and planned day four where I had to lay the foundation for my monument.

DAY 4

I called Vishnu again to drive us around the city. He picked me up in the morning and then drove to Tanishq's place.

Since none of us were driving, we decided to get day drunk. Vishnu brought us a bottle of vodka and we took neat shots in the back seat. Vishnu played the Bhojpuri songs at full volume and we danced. As the sun dropped down the horizon, we got tranced in alcohol. While dancing to the tunes of Bhojpuri songs, we experienced a close contact. Surrounded by the dim lights, I looked into her bright eyes. I wanted to kiss her and probably she felt the same. We moved closer to each other anticipating a kiss. I realized the plot wasn't vacant for me yet and a kiss at this point would be unfair and not so pious. The urge to kiss felt invalid and I withdrew my lips. She squeezed herself in my arms and I kissed her forehead. Once we sobered up, I dropped her at her place.

"Thanks for this incredible day," she said as she stepped out of the royal chariot.

Before leaving, she kissed me on my cheek and ran inside her apartment building. I was surprised and gently rubbed my lucky cheek. Vishnu rode me back to Sattu's place and throughout the journey, I smiled for no reason. With that peck on the cheek, I was assured that I had laid the foundation of my love.

DAY 5

On the most crucial day, I decided to go for a home run. I planned to express all my feelings verbally. In the past four days, I had expressed it enough through my actions. She called me before the meeting and said she wanted to talk. We decided to meet at a mall where we could sit and talk.

We sat in the coffee shop. She wore a beautiful hairband and I wondered whether it was the hairband that made her hair look beautiful or was it her hair that made that hairband look good. I was busy analyzing the hair and hairband when she broke the silence.

"You are leaving tomorrow," she said with moist eyes.

I nodded with my eyes fixed on the hairband.

"I need to say something very important," she said.

"What is that?" I said analysing the difference.

"Can you focus here?" she said holding my chin and repositioning my head. "Why did you come back?"

"I never left."

"Don't interrupt. Let me finish. I don't know what is happening since the time you are here. I have started to have second opinions about my existing relationship."

"That means…"

"Let me finish. I don't know what to do. There is Karan who doesn't value me at all. And then on the other end, it's you who does so much for me. I am so confused at the moment. Why do you love me so much?"

All this time I had been lying to her, but she had figured it out somehow.

"I don't love you," I said, controlling my emotions.

"You cannot even lie properly. Why do you love me so much?"

"Because you are Tanishq. You are the one whom I have loved madly and crazily. You are everywhere. I hallucinate. I see you everywhere. I am infected," I said as tears shed from my eyes.

"You are infected? What am I? A virus?" she said, hitting my hand.

"Worse than that. The virus has a cure, but you don't even have a cure. Once someone is charmed by you, he… he is gone forever."

She laughed while tears were still in her eyes.

"That is the worst thing I have heard about me."

"I tried to say the best things, but you cannot digest good things."

"That doesn't mean you stop saying good things."

"What do you want?" I asked her point blank.

"I don't know. I am confused. I was happily living my life and then you ruined it and now here I am in tears."

"That is how I was living since the last one year – in tears."

"I didn't ask you to go to Canada. You left me alone here."

And our fight continued. We accused each other of breaking up with tears in our eyes.

"What do you want?" I screamed, when I couldn't take it anymore. I was dying to know the conclusion.

"I want you to stop loving me," she replied calmly.

"Not possible."

"Why not?"

"Why can't you love me instead?"

"Not possible."

"Why not?

"Because I have someone in my life."

"Who doesn't value you at all?"

"Whatever. He is my boyfriend and I cannot cheat on him."

"Then don't argue with me."

We fought for over three hours. It was the last day and I wanted it to be memorable. It was hard to convince her and I gave up.

"Fine," I said, wiping my tears. "I will leave tomorrow and I will not ever contact you. I will try to forget you."

"Thanks."

"Can we live next few hours in peace, please?" I said as I paid for the coffee.

"Sure," she said.

We walked around the mall. She showed me her favorite shops. We entered a jewellery shop which was amongst her favorite stores.

"Look at that anklet," she said. "Isn't that pretty?"

She picked up the anklet and tried to put it on.

"Isn't that pretty?" she asked.

"You are pretty."

"Abby!" she warned me.

"Yes, it is."

She flipped over to see the price. It was expensive for her, but she didn't want to show me.

"But I have one of these," she said and put it back.

I noticed her checking the price and reacting to the price tag.

While she was checking other items, I grabbed the anklet and secretly passed it to one of the salesgirls along with my credit card. I asked her to pack it for me.

Even though I was strictly warned by her, I didn't stop loving her. One more hour was left for that day to end. I wanted to take one more chance.

Why?

Because love dies, but hope doesn't.

The Missing Piece

The fifth day came to an end. We decided to take a cab back home. I dropped her at a place from where she was supposed to walk home.

"Alright Abby," she said as she opened the door. "I guess that is it."

I sat in a grumpy mood refusing to say goodbye.

"Abby, please. I am leaving. Please give me a smiling goodbye," she said as she grabbed my forearm.

I didn't smile. Instead, I was trying my best to control my emotions. I looked in the opposite direction outside the window of the car.

"I am leaving then. Take care and go back with a smile. No more tears."

She got down from the cab and closed the door. I saw her through the window. She turned back and caught me staring at her. I pretended I didn't care and asked the cabbie to drive. He drove for a few hundred meters when I asked him to take a U-turn. He dropped me at the same place. I opened the door, got down and shouted.

"Tanishq!"

She came back running and we hugged. It was the most passionate hug. She cried and hugged me tight. I closed my eyes to immortalize the moment.

"Abby, please take care of yourself. I cannot see you this way," she said sobbing.

I nodded. I didn't want to leave her, but the people around made it awkward. I stepped back and looked around. I looked at the moon. It was at its best. It was a full moon night, with clouds all over.

A full moon night, a cold breeze and a drizzle – it makes probably the world's most beautiful triad that has the power to incubate love in any human heart. Nature was by my side, but not time. Time was running at twice its normal speed.

"I will leave now," said the beautiful Tanishq moving away from me.

"Can I walk with you?" I said scratching my stubble.

"It is a ten-minute walk. If you can spare that much energy, you're most welcome." Tanishq challenged pointing towards the road that led to her house.

I knew these were the last ten minutes I could spare with the love of my life. Without wasting any time I paid the cabbie and ran towards her. The goal was set in mind. I wanted to express my love, with an anticipation of acceptance.

Nature's beautiful triad was lending complete support to me, although my past was against it. Tanishq's mindset was another rival. We walked quietly for a while.

"Promise me you won't behave the same way once you go back home," Tanishq broke the ice.

"I promise I won't," I said making a cute puppy face. "I just thought I would be a better person if you are with me."

"Abby please," Tanishq grumped. "I have told you thousands of times. It is impossible. Why don't you understand?"

"Do we have any lame chance of getting together? Can Abby and Flabby be one all over again?" I threw my proposal close to a thousandth time.

"Abby, please! Can we just walk? Tonight is the last time we are together. I don't want to be rude to you. Please walk me home and leave."

I followed her command, rested my vocal cords and focussed on my feet to walk with her.

Tanishq held my right hand with her left one. I was surprised.

"Is nature's triad working? Is she convinced? Has she fallen for me?" My mind popped over zillion thoughts with that tactile sensation.

Before I could come to a conclusion, she put a brake on my mind's thought popping process.

"Come to this direction, we need to cross the road," she said pulling my right hand.

"Seriously, you held my hand to help me cross this road?"

"Of course, now run," she said, pulling me to synchronise my feet movement with hers.

Thanks to the traffic, she knew the Canadian guy cannot cross the Indian roads on his own.

On the other side of the road… Tanishq kept holding my hand.

For her, it was just a road crossing. For me, it was a moment of a lifetime. I felt the softness of her palm with my index finger. I then moved my finger to her ring finger. With my thumb and index finger, I felt her ring finger. Human physiology says that a nerve connects the ring finger to the heart. I was trying to feel that connection with her heart. Stupidly, I kept caressing her ring finger, anticipating a communication with her heart.

She was probably aware what I was up to, but decided to keep mum.

"I feel so lucky that I met you," she finally volunteered to break the silence.

I didn't reply to what she said. I was busy finding the physiological route to her heart.

"Where are you lost, Abby?" she said again.

I swayed my hand away from her. I walked three steps ahead of her and spontaneously turned towards her. We were standing on the roadside kerb.

I faced her and she was confused.

I bent down on my left knee. She was still surprised.

I spread my arms. She stood surprised.

She was worried about the act that had invited unwanted spectators all around. It wasn't the right spot for her as it was close to her house. It wasn't a right spot for me either, as by mistake, I had placed my knee on a broken piece of glass. It was uncomfortable for me, not to mention painful. Despite being in the wrong spots, we both decided to remain unmoved. I closed my eyes, took a deep breath and spoke my heart out.

"How much I love you, I need not to express again. You want me to stay happy? I will be. You want me to get my life together? I will. I am arranging all the jigsaw pieces of my life. I will one day earn big dollars and own the lifestyle I have always desired. I will find a girl and marry her. Probably I will be happy with that girl. I will rearrange the pieces. I might succeed in solving the jigsaw puzzle of my life. But a piece of my perfect jigsaw puzzle will always be missing. And that piece will be you. Without you, the puzzle will always be incomplete. I will be happy, but will always regret that missing piece. My chase for my dreams will successfully come to an end, but my quest for that missing piece will have no end."

Tanishq put her hands over her face. She was no more worried about the unwanted spectators. She looked into my moist eyes. A tear rolled down her beautiful cheeks.

I put my right hand into my pocket and took out the silver anklet – the one she couldn't buy at the mall.

"Don't worry, it is not the engagement ring." I winked and bent forward to hook the anklet on her left ankle. She stood surprised. She leaned forward to hug me and kissed on my neck.

"Thanks," she said with a cute characteristic nasal tone that follows tears. She helped me back on my feet. As expected, the denim had ripped off from the knee area and blood oozed from the skin underneath. I hid my sore knee to find a cure for my sore heart.

"I think I should leave now. Take care," she said as she hugged me.

This was probably the last hug between us. I closed my eyes and rested my chin on her shoulder and held her from the waist.

The drizzle transformed into rain. It was probably heaven crying over the unsuccessful love story. We both hid our tears under the downpour.

Tanishq moved back and I left her waist. It seemed like the angel had slipped from my hands. I couldn't say anything. I looked at her for one last time. Even though it was cloudy, the moonlight managed to escape the dense clouds and spread its limelight over her beautiful face. Her moist eyes were seeking answers to many unanswered questions. Her marvellous red lips urged to say goodbye. The winds blew the droplets away from her face. The dense black hair swayed at their best. Tanishq made everything look beautiful. And then, she left.

The moment she left, nothing was beautiful anymore. Not even the world's most beautiful triad. I stood alone, cursing the rains for creating a slush on the kerb. The moonlight wasn't enough to guide me to my destination and the breeze… the breeze brought dust and sand into my eyes.

I realized it was the missing piece that made everything perfect. The most beautiful triad that was being praised moments ago was cursed as the missing piece left. The roads ran off with slush, dust and darkness.

One Last Shot

Maybe in our next birth...

Tanishq sent me the last message.

She made it clear that I didn't have any chance with her in this birth. She assured me we would reincarnate and be with me. That would have sounded very idiotic, but every idiocy makes sense when you are hopelessly in love. I agreed to her next birth pact but that agreement had some conditions applied. We would not talk ever. She asked me to stay away from her.

I packed my bags and that very evening had to board a flight back to Canada. In the morning, I called Madiha to arrange for a ride from the airport to the university. I had not contacted her since her hearing with the dean. I didn't know what the verdict was, but one thing was sure – DC are very rarely student favoring. I called her.

"Hey. How are you?" I said in a soft voice.

"Hey, I am perfectly fine. How are you? How is the vamp? Did she say yes? Or are you still begging like a dog?" she said eagerly.

She bombarded me with a series of questions, and surprisingly, sounded excited. I was still worried about her DC verdict and before I could answer her questions, I decided to ask her about the verdict.

"What happened on the DC?"

"DC was great. I got to meet the dean and he is very sexy. I was surrounded by the beasts of the university. Banks was there too."

"What was the verdict?" I asked again.

"Remember the deadly bomb blast in Lahore last month?"

"What's new? Isn't there a bomb blast every other day in Pakistan?"

"Shut up! Nothing mean about my country," she said defensively.

"I am sorry, what about those?"

"My father's business got ruined in the blasts. His factories were blown apart and he suffered severe financial losses."

"What the hell? Why didn't you tell me that?" I was shocked knowing about her condition. She never let me know what she was going through.

"Take it easy. This is the story I cooked in my defence. As a result, I wasn't able to focus on my studies. I tried my best and survived the exams, but the last day was terrible and I couldn't finish my assignment. That's why I asked for your help and copied your assignment."

"They brought this story?"

"A beautiful girl with tears in her eyes has the superpower to win any battle. The dean fell for it. Banks brought it. They googled the bomb blast sites. I was set free on emotional and ethical grounds. They extended the assignment deadline for me and I resubmitted it."

"Congratulations beautiful girl."

"What is the verdict of your mission? Did the vamp say yes?"

"Nah, not really."

"What does that mean?"

"She said we cannot be together, at least not in this birth. But maybe in the next six births we can be."

"Are you dumb or what? I jeopardized my career for this idiotic mission and you are coming back with this shit. If you don't want to respect your efforts, then at least respect mine. Do you have any idea what all I have suffered for that bitch?"

Madiha lost her cool and swore at Tanishq. All that looked so valid and that is why I didn't stop her.

"You Indians leave everything for the next birth. Bloody procrastinators."

"Now you are being mean about my country. You are crossing the limits."

"You don't say a word. What is the guarantee you will take another birth."

"We believe we are born seven times as human beings."

"What if this is the seventh birth?"

She left me wondering. Her words echoed for a long time.

I had four hours before the final boarding. The airport was an hour away from Sattu's place. Without calculating the time, I grabbed my luggage and bid my goodbye to Sattu and his wife. He was supposed to drop me at the airport. I asked him to drop me to Tanishq's place instead.

"Dude, are you mad? It is the hottest day in the last sixty years. The outside temperature is forty-eight degree Celsius," Sattu said.

"I don't care. I need to clarify something," I said, stuffing my luggage in his car trunk.

"Since the last five days, you are trying to clarify things. Is there anything left?" Sattu asked.

I decided not to answer anything.

"Have some self-respect. That girl treats you like a dog. If not for yourself, for me, please have some self-respect."

"One last time. I feel like I cannot live without her."

"All this is bullshit. Spare your heart this pain. Let her go."

"I am doing this for my heart."

Sattu didn't say anything after that. He drove me right in front of her house and left.

In the afternoon, under the hot sun, I stood outside her house wearing the black shirt that she liked the most on me. She refused to pick my phone call. I left hundreds of messages to her and she came outside, all mad, her face red in anger.

"Why cannot you just leave?" Tanishq yelled.

"I came here to clarify something."

"I am done with your hopelessly in love saga. I am leaving unless you have something better to say."

"It is something better... I mean... I am not a hundred percent sure, but what if this is the last of our seven births."

"I am done with this," she said exasperated.

Sweat was dripping off her face and an idiot was bugging her for something she didn't want. Both the heat and the idiot had made her terribly cranky.

"It is time for some tough talk," she said, softening her voice. "We are never going to be together. I made up the bullshit next birth theory to calm you down, but you are so overly optimistic that you cannot help believing in that. You have to stop being stubborn. Go back home and we will never talk again."

"Years later, when this love story will be retold, I don't want people to say I failed because I didn't give it one last shot," I said.

"Come out of your virtual world. Years later, this won't be a love story; it will be a story titled how to be dumb and senseless."

"I like that title too, but..."

She stopped me in between and showed me her right index finger, raising her brow, indicating me to stop or else she would kill me.

"Please don't..." I tried to speak back.

"Please, Dr Shiva. Leave me alone. If you really love me and care for my happiness, never ever attempt to contact me. This story is over."

She left leaving me alone. I couldn't feel more helpless. The sun right on top of my head soaked the energy out of me. I tried one last shot and I gave up. The love, the hope, and the feelings all vanished in one moment. I called a cab and left for the airport.

The mission was over. The soldier had failed. The reward was tears and years of heartache.

Nobody Does That

Love is certainly the most unpredictable entity in this world. At a certain point you think everything is going in your favor, the next moment you are hit with reality and realize what happened was a myth.

What happened in the last five days was an illusion. The aftermath of those five days brought upon two different emotions. I thought I had won Tanishq's heart once again. Tanishq, on the other hand, was relieved that she won't get another chance to see the creepy lover.

My joy was turned down by Tanishq's rude behavior following my crazy outburst and she decided not to talk to me ever again. She abstained from contacting me, and to validate her decision she deleted my contact information from her phone book and blocked me from all the social networking sites.

I was again twelve thousand kilometers away from the love of my life. The same distance that had killed the relationship a year ago.

I tried to bring my life to normal.

Before I had left for India, my friends had made me take the oath. I had to prove to them that I was faithful to the promise.

Ming and Madiha came to pick me up at the airport along with another friend Sarah, who was now Ming's girlfriend.

"Yoohoo!" All of them shouted as they saw me exiting the airport gate.

"Hello everybody," I shouted with a smile, as fake as possible. "Gosh, so many people to pick me up."

"Yes, we all were dying to meet you."

"Me too. Come on everyone, give me a hug." I said as I hugged everyone.

"Who is she?" I asked another girl.

"Nandu, meet Casey, a new member of our gang," Madiha said.

"We brought a desperate white chick to hook you up," Ming whispered in my ear.

"Not again guys, let me breathe," I whispered back.

"Let's go to the car," Ming said carrying my luggage. "Oops! With the luggage on the back seat, there is no room for you."

"Idiots. You guys are such idiots. What was the need to bring this white chick?" I yelled at Madiha in Hindi to keep the conversation private.

"We are so sorry. But I have a plan. You and Casey sit here and have some coffee. We will drop your luggage and bring the car back," Madiha suggested.

"Now I got it. You guys aren't that dumb to bring a packed car and a desperate white chick," I said, yet again in Hindi.

"Have fun and focus on the remedy. This white skin is like Betadine on your wounds. Apply some," Madiha whispered in my ears.

"Alright, we will be back soon. Enjoy with Casey," she said, waved towards us and left.

I sat with Casey at the airport restaurant and chatted for around an hour before my friends came back to pick me up, this time with space in the car.

"Hello, friends. How was it?" Madiha said with a big smile.

"Well, I guess you should ask the lady," I said, directing them to Casey.

"Did you like our friend?" Madiha asked Casey.

"I give your friend a middle finger," Casey yelled, grabbed her bag and left in anger.

The moment she was invisible to us, I laughed maniacally. Ming and Madiha were angry and gave me a few mock punches for acting up yet again in front of Casey.

Tanishq met her old friend who was very well aware of the great Indian visit of her ex-boyfriend.

"So, how was meeting your ex again?" asked Priyanka, Tanishq's friend.

"The C-guy," Tanishq laughed.

"Hahaha, poor guy. Did he discover you saved his contact as C-guy?"

"Yes, he did. He was confused for a minute but I convinced him C means Canada," Tanishq laughed.

"What a dumb guy! Did he buy that?" Priyanka asked controlling her laughter.

"Of course, he did. He is too dumb and is always convinced with whatever I say."

"That's not dumb honey, that's trust." Priyanka stopped laughing.

"Get real. In today's world, that's called being dumb." Tanishq disagreed with her friend.

"I have seen you so happy after a long time. Are you sure he is not the reason behind this happiness?"

"Oh Lord! I am happy because he left India. I am in peace," Tanishq replied.

"Don't be so mean."

"You don't know how annoying he was. Came here to see his friends and family and all he did was stayed in Delhi and met me every single day. He lied to his parents."

"Jesus!"

"Yeah, and you won't believe what all he did. He brought an anklet for me that I really liked but could not afford. He surprised me with that and in front of around a hundred people went on his knees to present me that anklet. I mean, can you believe that! Wrote poems, bought me gifts and the last day was crazy. *Kkkrazzzzy*! It was really hot and that hopeless romantic was in front of my house at three in the afternoon. Not only that, he was dressed in black and was sweating all over. I asked why in black, and he said because I had always liked him in black. I mean grow up! You are taking so much pain for someone who doesn't even like you. You are on your knees without worrying about what people are thinking, bending in front of a girl to express your love and making a complete fool out of yourself. I mean who fucking does that?"

"Nobody," Priyanka replied.

"Exactly, nobody does that."

"No sweetheart, nobody does that."

"What do you mean?"

"Nobody does that for a girl. Especially for the one who doesn't care for those feelings. My boyfriend doesn't even come out in an AC car to see me if it is sunny outside. He was there standing on his feet in forty-eight degrees. Guys feel shy to claim that they have a girlfriend and he was publically on his knees making a complete fool of himself just to let the world know how much he loves you. Sweetheart, nobody, does that."

Tanishq was speechless for a moment. Priyanka squeezed her beautiful cheeks and left.

"Nobody does that!" Sarah said the same as I explained my crazy failure story to her. Madiha and Ming didn't want to listen to it and showed minimum interest. But Sarah being the new member of the group and a hopeless romantic like me paid scrupulous attention.

"You were on your knees for her!" she almost yelled.

"Height of stupidity," Madiha muttered.

"Here is the proud scar on my knee that's the sole witness to my efforts."

"You are crazy, Nandu. How do you do that? Who drives in a tunnel that has no light at the end?" Sarah said.

"When you don't care about the light and all you see is that beautiful smile that has always been the reason for your happiness, then you drive through the tunnel. When all you can see is that angel feeling special, you drive through the tunnel. When you see..."

"Stop it," Sarah interrupted in between. "What else did you do?"

After explaining all my crazy diary of events and after getting two hundred odd 'Nandu-you-are-a-Dumbo' from Madiha and Ming, I realized that no matter how much your friends try to convince you, no matter how much your brain is fed up with you, no matter how many white chicks you lose, you don't give up. You try, try and try. You hold on to it. You fight till the last breath. You fight with the broken knees, ripped heart and shattered hopes. You do every possible thing to find the missing piece. You do the crazy things over and over again that people refer to as "nobody does that!"

Epilogue

The eventful summer break came to an end. The university schedule kept me engaged and helped me cope up with the damage I had done to myself over the summer. I pretended to live a normal life and wore a smile in order to hide the void.

Every time my phone beeped, I was full of hopes. Most of the times, I was wrong, but I didn't stop believing. One night I received a phone call from an unknown number.

"Hello." I said.

"I didn't expect you to give up so easily."

"Tanishq?"

"Is there anyone else who can call you at this time?"

"How... I mean what... where... how are you?" I said perplexed as I could not believe my ears.

"Calm down," she said. "Have some water. I am absolutely fine."

"I never expected a phone call from you."

"And I never expected you to give up so easily."

I travelled thousands of kilometers so that I could see her, punched a man twice my size, roasted myself in heat, almost ruined my career, nearly lost all my friends, got deemed a fool – all this for one girl. And this girl says I gave up so easily!

The excitement of receiving her phone call soon transmuted to resentment.

"Didn't you see what made me give up? Do you even realize what I went through?" I said raising my tone.

"Listen…"

"No! I have listened to enough. Today, you listen to me! I have been too nice to you. I have done enough for you and more than enough to get you back into my life. If I had done even half of this for some other girl, she would have felt like the most special girl on earth. But you take me for granted. Anything I do for you is always less than what is required."

"Listen…"

"I am not listening to anything. It is not with you, it is with every girl. The one who is nice and polite gets thrashed and ignored. The one who cheats and treats you like trash is the one who deserves all the love and attention. You will try your best to find good in bad, but will not put in any attempt to seek that goodness from the good. You will cry your eyes out for the one who constantly breaks your heart, but will break the one who is trying to heal you. The bad ones are worth all the efforts and the good ones are just shoulders to cry on. There is more than just a shoulder in the nice ones. And that is their heart. A pure heart which has enormous love for you, but is scared to express because it knows, once it expresses itself, there is a series of rejections followed by pain and agony. It will be rejected with a conspicuous explanation that you are not ready and it will be broken. Soon after, it will see you gearing up for heartbreak, because you have found the new 'bad one'. You will be back, again, looking for a shoulder to cry on and rant how all men are the same. But you know what! They are not. Next time, try a nice man and see what he is capable of doing."

"I am sorry," she said softly.

"You better be."

"I agree I made a mistake, but I realized what I am missing. It has been so many days I wanted to contact you, but I could not gather courage. The temporary happiness made me oblivious of what is around me. Now that I am over that euphoria, I know what I want and I am sure about it."

"Why should I believe you?"

"Abby, I love you."

"When I said the same thing a few months ago, you didn't trust me. I moved mountains for you and it was still not enough. Why should I believe you?" I was angry.

"I can do anything to prove myself. Wait!"

From the background traffic noise, it seemed like she was on a busy road, probably on her way to work.

"Can you hold this phone?" Tanishq said to a random passerby.

She put the phone on loudspeaker and gave it to the passerby to hold.

"I am arranging all the jigsaw pieces of my life. I will one day own the lifestyle I always desired. I will find someone and marry him. Probably I will be happy with him. I will rearrange the pieces. I might succeed in solving the jigsaw puzzle of my life. But a piece of my perfect jigsaw puzzle will always be missing. And that piece will be you. Without you, the puzzle will always be incomplete. I will be happy, but will always regret letting that missing piece go. My chase for my dreams will successfully come to an end, but my quest for that missing piece will have no end."

I smiled over her vague reconstruction of my own speech. But I was enjoying the long due attention and didn't want the smile to ruin the moment.

"Very original. I am impressed," I said sarcastically.

"Please Abby, I am on my knees and my arms are spread wide open. I haven't done this for anyone in my life."

"Are you on your knees? Seriously!"

"Yes, she is on her knees spreading her arms," said the man who was holding her phone in front of her.

"I did not ask you, but thanks. What is this Tanishq? Get up from there. Don't make a fool out of yourself."

"Let me do it once. It is my turn to prove myself. I want to do it for you to make you realize how much you matter to me," she said, her voice cracking with emotions.

As much as I was enjoying the moment, I was also worried about her being on her knees in front of the crowd. What she did made me feel special.

"I love you." She shouted.

Those three words healed all the pain that I had gone through over the years.

"She is so beautiful. Brother, if you are not interested, can I try?" The man holding the phone said with innocence.

"You shut up and keep holding the phone," I yelled at the man as he was ruining the dream for me. "Tanishq, get up, and please take your phone from him."

"Once I get the answer, I will get up."

"I love you too. Now please get up from there."

"I didn't hear it properly."

"I love you too." I literally screamed.

"Ok bhaiyaji. Now you may leave. Thank you very much." She took possession of her phone and let the passerby go.

"Now you know how painful it is to be on your knees for someone. How many times have I done that for you," I said.

"It was not painful for the knees. I was worried about my new jeans. It was getting dirty," she replied, dusting off her jeans.

"Seriously! A jeans is more important than my feelings. I don't want to talk."

"I am joking."

And the fights continued...

Tanishq is back in my life and so is the glee. I introduced her to all my friends. Ming likes her and narrates all the stories that we live in the class. Sarah calls her the luckiest girl on the planet. And Madiha only pretends to like her. She still calls her vamp for what she did to me and for getting her close to being expelled. Fair enough! Every time Tanishq tries to strike a conversation with her, she makes a subtle excuse and leaves. This prompts me to coin a new theory —'Two beautiful girls can never be good friends'. I showed a picture of Tanishq and revealed 'the other side' to Dr Yeomans, and she said it was worth creating history for. Like all good things, it took some time, but in the end, it was all worth it. The most desirable missing piece fit perfectly into the jigsaw puzzle.

Nice men do not finish last. They might not get what they want, but they surely get what they deserve. Not everyone deserves the kind of heart you have. It takes a special person to realize the worth of goodness.

Keep believing… you nice man.